# Song
# of the Rock

Also by Don Coldsmith

THE SPANISH BIT SAGA

RIVERS WEST: THE SMOKY HILL

# Song
# of the Rock

》》 》》 》》 》》 》》 》》 》》 》》 》》 》》 》》 》》

## DON COLDSMITH

A Double D Western
**Doubleday**
NEW YORK   LONDON   TORONTO   SYDNEY   AUCKLAND

A Double D Western
Published by Doubleday, a division of
Bantam Doubleday Dell Publishing Group, Inc.
666 Fifth Avenue, New York, New York 10103

Double D Western, Doubleday,
and the portrayal of the letters DD
are trademarks of Doubleday, a division of
Bantam Doubleday Dell Publishing Group, Inc.

Library of Congress Cataloging-in-Publication Data

Coldsmith, Don, 1926—
    Song of the rock/Don Coldsmith.—1st ed.
        p.   cm.
    I. Title.
PS3553.O445S6   1989
813'.54—dc19   89-31098
CIP

ISBN 0-385-24575-0
Copyright © 1989 by Don Coldsmith
All Rights Reserved
Printed in the United States of America
September 1989
First Edition
OG

W

Time period: Late 1600s, a few years
after *Trail from Taos*

# Song
# of the Rock

# 1
## » » »

Perhaps it would have happened anyway, the return to the old ways. Most of the People, however, were inclined to attribute the trend to the collapse of the trading in Santa Fe. For a generation trade had continued, and the People had benefitted greatly, exchanging furs, robes, and sometimes dried meat or pemmican for metal knives, tools, and blankets from the Spanish.

Then came the summer when the men of the pueblos revolted against Spanish rule, and drove the "metal people" all the way back to El Paso Del Norte, in Mexico. The hostilities put an end to the trading, and the People and their allies, the Head Splitters, withdrew to the wide skies of the prairie country.

The return to the old ways was part of the result. It was, in a way, necessary, because the modern conveniences of the metal people were no longer available. It was necessary to revive some of the almost outmoded customs and methods.

Along with this came a renewed interest in the understanding of things of the spirit. In this, the area of religious experience, none showed greater interest than young White Fox, son of Red Feather and Moonflower.

White Fox had been at a very impressionable age when he and his father were jailed by the Spanish. Hardly fifteen summers, he was taking part in his first trading journey. Only with great difficulty had the party from the plains managed to escape. The bones of two of their number would rest in the strange soil of the mountains, instead of returning to the life-giving sod of the prairie.

All of these things had made a deep impression on the young man. He continued to strive for skill in the hunt, but he also asked many questions. Deep, thoughtful questions about things of the spirit. He talked at great length with his father, Red Feather, and with his grandfather of the same name, the aging chief of the Eastern Band. He sought the knowledge of Pale Star, whose life experience was broader than any other of the People.

With great insight, Star perceived that here was a young man whose spirit cried out for knowledge. She encouraged him to talk with Looks Far, the highly respected medicine man of the Southern Band. The old man was pleased to see a youngster of his own band take such interest, especially one who was practically family. Looks Far had seen with alarm the trend away from things of the spirit, as greater interest in the trade route to Santa Fe had permeated a generation. He had been almost pleased over the collapse of the southwest trade.

And now, he was greatly pleased. He hoped that this interest would blossom and bear fruit. He was beginning to fear that no young man would aspire to the office of medicine man. This generation seemed far more interested in trading with the Spanish, and he feared the foreign influence.

It was always a pleasure to see a young person who asked questions. He remembered Pale Star as a child, and how she had asked many questions. Now came this young White Fox. Looks Far was aware of the boy's brush with death at the hands of the Spanish. Sometimes such an experience would startle a person into inquiry as to the nature of things. Possibly, even, White Fox could be one who would receive the gift of spiritual insight, which would make him a medicine man. He could not suggest such a thing to White Fox. The boy would have to seek it for himself. It was possible, even, that if the gift was offered, White Fox would refuse the call. It was not unusual to refuse the honor of such a gift because of the heavy responsibility that it carried.

So, Looks Far realized, he must not push the young man. He would be available to him, ready to answer questions. He might even suggest that White Fox go on a vision-quest. Many of the young men were neglecting that important spiritual experience, in this generation. Their quest followed more along the lines of the southwest trade. Their interest lay in the best knives, lance points, and arrowheads, rather than things of the spirit. A few, of course, followed the old way, and sought their spirit-guide through the fasting and prayer of the vision-quest. Still, it was disheartening that many capable warriors did not.

The time might come when Looks Far could suggest a vision-quest to young Fox, but not yet. It would be better for him to seek it on his own. No one could seek a vision-quest for another, anyway.

So, Looks Far bided his time and watched White Fox grow, spiritually as well as physically. The lanky frame was filling out with hard flat muscle, the boyish voice deepening. Fox began to have enough facial hair to pluck with the clam shells. Still his curiosity deepened, and he often sought out Looks Far for discussion. Thus the announcement was no great surprise to Looks Far when it came.

"Uncle," White Fox began one afternoon, "I would seek a vision-quest."

Ah, thought Looks Far, it is good. And Fox had even broached the subject himself. Looks Far's heart was full of joy, but he tried to maintain his dignity.

"Yes, my son, where will you go?" he asked seriously.

It would be necessary to go far enough so that no one would

accidently blunder in and disturb the seeker. The band had camped on Sycamore River for the summer after the end of the Big Council. It was an area that they had used before, one of their favorite sites for summer camp. Looks Far was also aware that a day's travel upstream was the locale of Medicine Rock. It was a spiritual place of great importance. It was here that long ago a man called Eagle had spent the winter in a cave. Eagle was honored in song and dance because of his strange spiritual experience at the rock. He had become, not a medicine man, but a skilled storyteller. It was said that he could tell stories of Creation as if he had been there.

Some felt that Medicine Rock was a place of evil, but Looks Far had never thought so. Probably it was a place of the spirits, a sacred place. The People had always refrained from camping too close because of its spiritual nature, and the reluctance to disturb such a place.

These very factors would seem to make it an ideal place for a vision-quest, however. Looks Far waited for White Fox to inquire about a site for his quest. Then he would suggest Medicine Rock.

The young man paused for a long time before answering.

Looks Far was on the verge of asking again when Fox finally spoke.

"I had thought maybe I would go to Medicine Rock."

The old medicine man could hardly contain his excitement. *Aiee*, what a good sign! A sensitive spirit like that of White Fox, in touch with those of the Rock! With difficulty, Looks Far maintained his dignity, and took a long draw on his pipe before answering.

"Yes," he said calmly. "It is good."

# 2

>> >> >>

**W**hite Fox stood on the south side of the river and stared up at the gray cliff known as Medicine Rock. He had never been this near it before, having only seen its dark line in the distance, looming above the tops of the trees along the river. In reality, it was not a rock, but a bluff which marked the river's course along its north bank for perhaps half a day's journey. From where he stood he could see that in both directions, the cliff tapered toward the level of the riverbed.

He scrutinized the face of the rock for a path to the top. He could camp here, he supposed, but somehow he felt that one's vision-quest should be on some high place, from which he could watch the movement of the sun, the moon, and the stars.

Upstream, perhaps a long bow shot, it appeared that there was a rift or crevice in the cliff, and he moved in that direction, chewing a piece of dried meat as he did so. Soon he would begin his fast, but until then, he would need his strength. Still chewing, he put the last bit of meat back in the pouch at his waist. He had a purpose for it.

He crossed the river at a shallow riffle that murmured over white gravel, and stopped to drain the water out of his moccasins on the other side. There was a suggestion of a path along the narrow strip of soil that separated the river from the rock, and he followed it toward the crevice. In retrospect much later, he was to think that there may have been something odd about a game trail in this location. He thought nothing of it at the time, however. He was too concerned about finding a way to the top. He paused to drink his fill, and filled his waterskin.

The trail did lead into a broken rocky crevice which sloped upward into the cliff. It was a wound, it appeared, which might have been hacked into the cliff by a giant ax. The broken fragments of stone which spilled out of the cleft were tumbled out into the river itself, where dark water swirled around dark boulders. The stones were of a convenient size, and he began to climb, stepping from one boulder to the next. Again, it did not occur to him that this game trail was almost too easy. There was dense growth of fragrant sumac and prairie dogwood on either side, but none to impede his progress.

About halfway up, something white caught his eye to the left, and he paused to look. There below him was a pocket in the crevice, tightly packed with bones. Bones of all sizes. A chill caught at him, and prickled the hairs at the back of his neck. What was this strange occurrence? For a moment, he thought of retreating, but common sense held him. There must be some reasonable answer to this jumbled pile of bones. He sat down on a boulder and studied the situation. Meanwhile he began to recognize more bones among the rocks. Buffalo bones, mostly, though he identified a horse's skull. All of the bones were bleached and weathered.

Then he remembered. Aside from the story of the spirit-experience of Eagle, there was another story of Medicine Rock. A gener-

ation or two ago . . . what was it? Ah, yes, invaders from the
north. Looks Far himself, as a young man, had joined his medicine
with that of a medicine man of the Head Splitters. They had
decoyed the dreaded invaders to this area and stampeded a buffalo
herd to push them over the cliff. Of course! In the ensuing years,
the river had carried away or broken to pieces the exposed remains
of the buffalo. But here in the crevices and crannies of the rocks,
the moldering bones could only lie through the seasons, hidden
away from the world.

He wondered a little about the rider of the unfortunate horse
whose bones lay below. Had he escaped? Or was he killed, and his
body removed? Possibly, even, his bones also moldered beneath the
bleaching pile of buffalo remains. Ah, well, that was long ago. He
rose, having solved the mystery to his satisfaction, as well as having
caught his breath. He climbed on.

He was above the tops of all but the tallest trees now. He could
pause and look up and down the river, and the view was magnifi-
cent. He was glad that he had chosen this spot for his vision-quest.
Its beauty made him eager to begin his fast, to enter into a oneness with the world. He climbed on.

At the top, puffing slightly, he climbed out onto the level stone
rim and stood to look around. The immediate area was as flat as
still water, and stretched away into the distance with only a gentle
roll. Even though the general lay of the land was what he had
expected, the appearance was startling. The level flat of the plain
came to the cliff's edge and simply dropped off. He could see now
how it had been possible to maneuver the enemy invaders into
position and crowd them over to their deaths.

The sun was lowering in the west, and he hastened to make
camp. A fire was essential, so he began to gather dead sticks from
some of the scrubby brush which clung to cracks in the rim of the
cliff. He took out his fire sticks, and with the fire-bow twirled the
yucca spindle to produce a glowing spark. Carefully he gathered it
on a pinch of tinder and breathed it into life. A flint and steel from

the Spanish trade would have been quicker, but it did not seem appropriate to the spirit of his vision-quest.

The little fire began to grow as daylight began to fade. He fed it meagerly. It was not necessary for cooking or warmth, but for ceremony. It was a ritual fire only, a declaration to the spirits of the place that "with your permission, here I intend to camp."

He spread his robe, gathering some of last year's dead grass to pad the sleeping-place, and sat down to watch the setting of the sun. He took out his last stick of dried meat and broke it equally in half. One part he solemnly deposited on the fire as a sort of sacrifice to whatever spirits might take notice here. The other he chewed slowly, the last morsel of food he would take until after his vision-quest was over.

The air was still, and the pleasant scent of roses drifted across the plain. The season was good, the grass green. Sounds of the day were fading, replaced by the sounds of the creatures of darkness. A coyote called from a distant hill, and its mate answered.

Below him, a fish splashed in the river. There was the hollow cry of Kookooskoos, the great hunting owl. How strange, to hear that sound from below him.

Stars began to appear in the darkening blue of the sky, and the world was good. Now, he knew, there was nothing to do but wait. He added a few twigs to the fire, and on an impulse stood to sing the Song of Fire, because it seemed an appropriate thing to do. Then he settled back down.

He did not feel sleepy at all. He was far too excited. The light faded to the strange blue-purple of twilight, which distorted not only distance but reality. There was an air of expectancy, a sense of some supernatural event about to happen. Then the great red disk of the full moon edged its way above earth's rim to the east, and the feeling of wonder and mystery was complete.

The red circle had shrunk to half its size and turned to silver overhead before White Fox finally drew his robe around him and lay down to sleep. He was a little disappointed. There had been nothing out of the ordinary. Only the accustomed night sounds and the silvering of earth with moonlight.

He lay waiting for sleep to come. The last sound he remembered before falling asleep was the slap of a beaver's tail on the surface of the river far below.

# 3

**》》 》》 》》**

**W**hite Fox awoke with the rising sun in his eyes, unsure where he was for a moment. Then he remembered and sat up in anticipation. But the magic of the night was gone now. The unearthly silver-blue of the moonlit world had been restored to the normal colors of any pleasant morning in the Moon of Roses. He looked up and down the river, and across the tops of the trees which lined its banks.

Through an opening in the vegetation, he saw a deer tiptoe her way gingerly to the water to drink, followed by a pair of spotted fawns. He smiled. Twins, a good sign. But no, another doe, somewhat more grayish-yellow than the reddish color of the first, came into sight. Ah, one of the young must belong to her. Then to his surprise, two more fawns tottered into view. *Aiee,* what good fortune! What a favorable omen, not only for his vision-quest, but for the season. Any season in which the does are prone to twinning will be a good year.

His stomach rumbled, calling attention to his fast.

"Be still," he said, "you have a long time to wait."

White Fox sipped a little water, and then rebuilt his fire, starting it from the tiny coals of last night's blaze. He walked to the rim of the cliff and performed the Morning Song, lifting his hands to the sky in the prayer of thanks for the new day. A few more sticks now fed the fire, and he spent a little while gathering more, moving a few steps back down the cliff path to reach a dead bush he had noticed there.

It was about that time that he noticed a strange sensation. He could not have described it, a sort of feeling that he was not alone. It was as if he were someone else, and himself as well, standing on the narrow path, his foot on a projecting rock to more easily reach the dry fuel. No, more like someone else had stood just this way. Or, as if someone watched him. He glanced around, half expecting to see someone, but he was alone. Only a bright-eyed sparrow balanced gracefully on a twig and watched him curiously. Watching the teetering bird, White Fox became dizzy for a moment. He leaned hard against the cliff until his head cleared.

What was it? The effect of his fast already? Maybe, he thought. He must be very careful about the treacherous path if dizziness was to be a part of his experience. He gathered the sticks he had dropped, and made his way back up to the rim.

The dizzy sensation was gone now, but there remained the memory of the other feeling, that he was not alone. That was a separate experience, not related to the dizziness, and one that was very real. *Aiee*, the spirits of this place must be very active! It whetted his eagerness.

His stomach growled again, and a hunger pang clawed through his abdomen. He took only a tiny sip of water. The waterskin was his only supply, without negotiating the path to the river and back. He hated to think of trying that. There were places on the narrow ledges that were dangerous, even without dizzy spells.

He sat down near the edge and looked again up and down the stream. The haze of fog in the river's bend was beginning to lift now, a thin layer of mist above the water's surface. It was interesting, the way he could see the tree trunks both above and below the layer of fog. Again, he heard the slap of a beaver's tail on the surface of the water. He remembered that from the night. Downstream a band of crows were angrily calling an alarm, and he watched in that direction. Soon a great owl came flying on quiet wings, softly slipping among the trees along the river. *Kookooskoos* was pursued by a raucous horde of noisy crows, who flapped and dived at their traditional enemy repeatedly.

White Fox smiled as he watched from above. The owl did not even lose its dignity. It sailed in a smooth glide, to rise at the end and land effortlessly on a dead snag near the cliff's face. From there it was only a short flight to a crevice where it disappeared from view. The owl's tormentors circled and cried in protest for a little while, but their game was over. They soon fell silent and went their separate ways.

White Fox, a little bored, settled back to wait. He was hungry, but that was expected for the first day of a fast. It would pass. For now, until he began to benefit from the anticipated visions, he would simply observe the world and enjoy it.

From this vantage point, as the fog melted and disappeared, he now found that he could see much of the river's course. It curled in deep pools against the dark gray of the cliff, murmured over white gravel bars, and among the knobby knees of the giant sycamores that knelt at the water's edge. He wondered idly just where the cave was located, the winter abode of the legendary Eagle. Did the injured youth look down on this same scene, the chalk-white bark of the sycamore there? Did the leaves of that very tree, a giant of many winters, murmur in conversation with the stream while Eagle listened, as Fox listened now? He realized that he was thinking in abstract terms, but after all, was that not the purpose of a vision-quest?

A beaver splashed again. Was this beaver family descended from those heard by Eagle as he lay in his cave, generations ago? Fox studied the river again. It was ideal for beaver. The deep pools made it unnecessary for them to even build a dam. He had not seen a beaver lodge as he approached last evening, but often the animals merely used a den in the riverbank itself in such a setting. Life would be easy here. The explosive slap of a tail on the water sounded again, and he smiled. It was startling, the loud crack of warning that the animals could make as they dived. It was apparent that many times there was no real danger, that the warning was only in play. The beavers could apparently alter the sound of the slap to fit the urgency of the situation.

He lifted his gaze to watch a red-tailed hawk, circling with fixed wings on the rising air that lifted as the sun began to warm the face of the cliff. It was good, he thought, to take these days to merely watch and learn of the earth and how its creatures lived. Maybe this was the goal of the vision-quest. But no, there must be more, a great deal more. He had had no visions yet. He wondered if they would come as dreams, the visions of sleep, and if so, would he be able to remember them when he woke? Sometimes such night-visions seemed quite real, and every detail could be remembered. Sometimes it was possible only to remember fragments. Then there are the terrifying night-visions that one sometimes has, when it is good to waken. He wondered what the effect of the fast would be on all of these. Looks Far had repeatedly mentioned the clarity that the fast brings. Would it help with the memory of the dreams? Or, would the vision-seeker be in an entirely different state, seeing and experiencing visions while not asleep?

He sighed deeply. He must not become impatient. It would come to him in due time, but he must wait for the effects of the fast. He had not dreamed at all last night.

But wait, he thought suddenly. Did I not dream? Was there not a time, after the moonlight turned silver-blue, when I woke . . . no, I was not awake, but I heard the beavers, and . . .

Flitting through the cobwebby recesses of his mind was an unclear picture, which seemed somehow to be part of his presence here in this place of spirits. There was, somehow, an interfering presence, a disharmony that had intruded, to jar the calm of his now-forgotten dream. He closed his eyes and strained to remember, but it was of no use. The memory of the fragmented dream was much like that of reality, the moonlight on the river, the night-sounds. But he had a strange partial recollection of something more ominous, something not a part of the night of magic. A face came into his memory, not remembered clearly, but in brief partial pictures. Long, unkempt hair, large burning eyes, and an expression on the face that was midway between fear and fury.

He opened his eyes in alarm. He was not even certain that this face was human. For an instant he thought of abandoning his vision-quest and fleeing this strange place, but then he calmed. He had never heard of anyone who abandoned a vision-quest. Certainly, not when it had hardly started. He would be ridiculed forever.

Besides, was it not the purpose of the quest to approach and learn of things of the spirit? He took a deep breath, and the cold prickling sensation at the back of his neck seemed to subside somewhat. In the clear air and the warming light of the sun, the chill of fear that had washed over him for a few moments seemed ridiculous.

Still, he wondered, is this thing of fear a part of the vision-quest? A gnawing doubt remained.

# 4

>> >> >>

The day was uneventful after the confusing thoughts with which it began. Except, of course, for the intermittent gnawing of his empty stomach. He did not know quite how to approach the time of sleeping, and had some dread of the poorly remembered dreams. He sat up by the fire, listening to the night-sounds and waiting for the moon to rise.

Moonrise was later, of course, and in the velvety blackness after sunset, he studied the scatter of stars, picking out constellations. The Seven Hunters, who nightly made a wide circle around their camp at the Real-star, were especially brilliant tonight. He could easily pick out the small star beside the next to the last of the Hunters. It was said to represent his dog.

In the distance, a coyote called, and another answered. There was the deep-throated challenge of a buffalo bull out on the prairie, and a far-off sound that may have been the cry of one of the big gray prairie wolves. Closer at hand was the repeated cry of a night bird, and down the river the hollow booming of one of the big green frogs that could sound like the bellow of a bull. A night-heron called, his short discordant chortle jarring to the ear.

White Fox decided that he was becoming more sensitive to the sounds of the night. The fast was said to do that. He had had only a sip of water a little before evening fell. With some degree of surprise he suddenly realized that he had had no hunger pangs for a while. That, too, was as he had been told, but still it surprised him. Next, he had heard, would come the clarity of thought that he was seeking. It certainly had not happened yet. In fact, he could not remember when to expect it, now. After a day, two days? He shrugged, and drew his robe around his shoulders against the chill of the prairie night. Below him he heard the beavers at play, and the splash and slap of their pretended warnings.

Finally the moon's edge began to show, and the night again was cloaked in mystery as the red-orange orb, now slightly flattened on one side, rose majestically to balance on Earth's rim for a moment before climbing on. It was as breathtaking as on the previous night, perhaps more so, with the influence of the mystical thoughts that had occupied him earlier. Maybe the effect of his fast was beginning to be felt, too; he could not be sure.

There was much about the fast and the vision-quest that could never be told. It was too personal a thing, something one could never share, because it was to be experienced, not described. He could understand that. However, he decided ruefully, it certainly made it difficult to know what to expect. Maybe everyone's vision-quest was different, he thought. There was no way to know, since a complete retelling of one's visions seemed almost forbidden. Yes, that must be it, he decided. Everyone's visions are different, and so it would be impossible to know what to expect, even if the experience of others had been told to you.

White Fox paused, not quite certain whether that logic was valid, or whether it merely seemed so because of . . . *aiee*, he thought, I must have some sleep . . . I am confusing myself. He rolled in his robe and lay down, to wait for sleep to come.

Again, he hardly expected to sleep, and again, dropped off almost immediately. He awoke with the rising sun, excited at the prospect of the day. He was already partway through his few chores with which to greet the day when he realized that he was moving with renewed intensity. It was a joy to be alive on such a day, and his Morning Song had never carried such enthusiasm. Yes, this was it, the expected intensity of all his senses, as he had been told to expect. He could hardly refrain from crying out with the pure enjoyment of it. He *did* cry out, a spontaneous shout of happiness that echoed up and down the river. The other creatures of the day seemed not to notice, for he was one with them.

Somewhat calmer, White Fox began to sort out his feelings. His senses were all more acute. Sounds, while not magnified, were more apparent to him. He could more easily identify and define the origin of sounds he had never noticed before. The rustle of insects in the tall grass, the distant hollow tapping of a woodpecker probing for insects in a dead cottonwood branch. He could clearly identify, and without effort, know the origins of each small sound.

Similarly, his eyesight seemed keener. Small details in the distance, once dimly visualized, became sharp and clear. Colors were more intense, yet at the same time he found that he could distinguish subtle shades of difference.

Most startling, however, was his awareness. The red-tailed hawk again circled on rising air, and as he watched the effortless spirals, he suddenly realized something that he had never felt before. He could know what the bird felt. It was not a thing that could be put into words, but an emotion that was present. Without knowing how it happened, he was aware of the hawk's feeling of flight, the air under her wings pushing her upward in another circle and another. He had tried before to imagine how it must feel to be an eagle, soaring high above Earth, but his imagination had fallen short. Now he knew. He had experienced flight. There was another feeling, too. He knew the hawk's concern for her two half-grown young in the nest at the top of the big sycamore downriver. He could have told exactly where the bird intended to hunt that morning, and the appearance of the grassy meadow from the air. For an instant, he was one with the thoughts of the hawk.

Delighted with the new experience, he tried to focus on other creatures' thoughts and feelings. The sound of the beavers below drew his attention. With little effort, he could sense the feel of the water sliding past the creatures' bodies as they swam smoothly through its coolness. There was a strong sense of safety in the water, but of potential danger above. He was aware, somehow, of the presence of a large fish, disturbed by the beavers, and caught the flash of fear as it turned aside, followed by realization and dull resentment at the intrusion. It was a poorly formed thought, and he noted it as appropriate to the lesser abilities of a fish.

His interest now probed the world around him. He felt the fear in the timid mouse that crouched unseen under a clump of grass a few paces away. The cheerful song of a bird nearby was now interpreted as a territorial challenge, a threat to intruders.

In the distance, a small herd of buffalo grazed, and his curiosity reached out to them. Here a strange feeling, a *herd* thought, came at him, calm, solid, a composite that simply had the feel of communal grazing. He found that he could move his thought from one to the other of the animals, to feel individual emotions. A yellowish calf displayed a moment of anxiety at being out of sight of its mother. The cow, in turn, realized the uneasiness and called softly. He had long known of these things, but had never *felt* them before. It was as if he could, almost at will, be inside the heads of the creatures. *Aiee*, what an experience!

He focused his attention on a gigantic bull, and was startled when the animal lifted its head and seemed to look directly at him. Its thought reached out, without words, but with a message startlingly clear.

"Welcome, my brother, to the secrets of the prairie."

For most of the day, White Fox enjoyed this newfound game. He seemed to slip in and out of reality, and there were times when he was not certain which was real and which was spirit. Although, he was now certain, both were real. The world of reality and the world of the spirit were *both* real, were both different phases of the same thing.

It was late in the day now, and the shadows were lengthening. White Fox was curious, trying to reach out to the spirits of the night creatures as they came awake. He had discovered that the process was somewhat more simple when he knew the location of the creature he sought. His concentration was easier. He was absently wondering what manner of creatures would be awakening from their lodges in the face of the rocky cliff. It was while he was absorbed in this that he suddenly encountered a sensation which drew his entire attention. A cold sweat dampened his skin, and the prickle at the back of his neck returned. He glanced fearfully around the little circle of light that marked the limits of his fire's illumination, but saw nothing.

It had been only a momentary thing, a flash that was gone, like the silvery flash of minnows as they dart into the depths of a still pool to disappear. This, of course, was not a visible thing, but one of the spirit. The shocking part was the unspeakably evil sensation that flashed through the mind of White Fox. A sense of some horrible, malevolent spirit out there somewhere in the darkness. Something with intelligence of a high order, yet not human. He had felt the dark thoughts of the snake stalking a bird's nest earlier in the day, but this was more than dark thoughts. There was inexpressible *evil* here.

There had been another flashing sensation at about the same moment, which was also quite brief, and which added to his confusion. It was an unmistakable sense of fear. Fear of that evil Thing whose spirit he had encountered unwittingly. He was certain that it was not his own fear, but that of someone else.

For the first time that day, he thought of the strange, nearly forgotten dreams of his first night on the rock. Could this possibly be connected with the creature he only half remembered in that dream?

White Fox searched his memory for fragments of anything he had ever heard about vision-quests. He could remember nothing remotely resembling this feeling. It was frightening, because he did not know what to expect. If this was a part of his vision-quest, so be it. Even though it was frightening, if he knew it was expected . . . but no, his suspicion was growing that this was not to be expected. If terror and evil were part of the vision-quest, it would be common knowledge, and he had never heard of such things.

No, he feared that something was dreadfully wrong here, an evil that had nothing to do with a vision-quest. Worse still, he had no idea what to do about it.

# 5

>> >> >>

The third night on the rock was marked by dreams. There are dreams which seem so real that, on awakening, one still half believes their reality. At other times, the dreamer knows, even as he dreams, that it is only a vision, and will be gone when he awakens. Sometimes he may view this, even at the time, as amusing, or, if the dream is pleasant, may regret that it must end.

However, White Fox's third night on the rock was unique. He dreamed with the sharpened senses of his vision-fast, so that every detail seemed crystal clear. The puzzling thing was that he was awake from time to time, and the visions seemed to continue. He found it impossible, in his vision-state, to distinguish whether these were actually dreams, common sleep-vision, or whether they were visions occurring during his periods of wakefulness. The entire night, and even the next morning, seemed to blur together as one continuum, an indistinguishable experience. He found later that the oneness continued in his memory also. He assumed that it was part of the vision-quest. It was exciting, exhilarating, joyful.

It was also a little frightening at times, and that seemed odd to him, even as it occurred. The vision-quest was expected to be an intense experience, as one became attuned to all of existence, became part of the world and the heavens. He did not remember that he had ever heard it described as frightening. But the fear was there, coming at him unexpectedly from time to time, jarring his sensibilities for a moment, to be gone the next. He had the odd feeling that, even though there seemed a oneness in all else, this was something outside. The thoughts of impending evil that intruded into his dreams or visions were just that. Intrusions. Yes, that was it. The evil thing, whatever it was, that generated fear in his spirit, was actually not a part of the vision-quest at all. It was something that was interfering with his quest.

He came to this conclusion during one of his wakeful periods in the night, and felt better for having sorted it out. He resolved to resist or deny the evil thing when it tried to obstruct the course of his visions.

That did not help. The next time the evil thing occurred, and White Fox thrust it from him, it seemed to become enraged. It was still a formless, nondescript feeling, with no appearance or shape, but its spirit came at him with an angry rush. He thrust it from him with a burst of anger of his own, and it crept away into the shadowy depths of his mind, with an unspoken promise that it would return.

White Fox woke, a cold sweat on his body, and still fearful, built up his fire a little. He thought of some discussions which he had heard about the Medicine Rock. It was thought to be a place of the spirits, but now he began to wonder. *Bad* spirits? Was this a place of evil, causing interference with his vision-quest? Was that why few had ever chosen to undertake their quest here?

But no, he was experiencing very satisfactory visions, good communication with the spirits of all living things. There was just this annoying, almost terrifying experience, which kept interfering. Still uneasy, he drifted back to sleep. If, indeed, there was any difference between sleep and wakefulness during that third night.

It was toward morning that his animal spirit-guide made itself known. He had heard the beavers splashing and cavorting in the river far below, and slipped into spirit-communion with them as he had done previously. His mind wandered, and he saw himself again sliding through cool moonlit waters with the beavers, or perhaps as one of them.

It seemed quite logical, then, to have one of the beavers accost him. Looking back at the experience later, he was never certain exactly where the confrontation took place. Logically, it should have been on the riverbank, but it could have as easily been at the rim of the cliff, or in the prairie somewhere. It was a meeting in which time and place were unimportant. Words, too, were unimportant. It was only later that he recalled that there had been no audible words, but a meeting of the spirits. So, while he could not have described the sound of the guide's voice, he felt deeply the dignity of its spirit.

It was by far the largest beaver he had ever seen, the grandfather of all beavers. The creature approached him, and White Fox seemed to look up at it, as if he were sitting. The beaver stopped and rocked back on its haunches and tail to sit erect, as a man squats by the fire. Fox was keenly aware of the brightness in the eyes, and the keen cutting edges on the long incisor teeth. He even remembered afterward the wriggle of the animal's nose and whiskers, like those of a rabbit eating clover. In a moment the significance of the meeting sank in.

"*You* are my spirit-guide?" he gasped.

"Of course. Have we not talked to you by the tail-slap?"

White Fox was embarrassed. He felt that he had appeared unappreciative.

"Yes, Grandfather, I did not know," he apologized.

The beaver cocked its head to one side.

"Yes, that is true. But, we have been concerned for you. There is danger here."

"For your people, Grandfather?"

"No, no. For you. There is evil here. You must take care."

White Fox was slightly irritated. His spirit-guide, he had thought, would provide him with some answers. Instead, it was only verifying the existence of the questions.

"But what . . ." he began, but the beaver held up a paw to interrupt.

It was becoming indistinct now. Fox was afraid that he had offended his spirit-guide, and it would now abandon him.

"Do not leave me," he pleaded. "What must I do?"

"Look around you, look and learn. We will help you."

"But, Grandfather, I . . ."

But the beaver was gone. White Fox now fell into another period of dream-sleep (or remained in one, he was never certain). It was a troubled dream, and he once more saw the face he had seen when he spent the first night on the rock. The same unkempt hair, the burning dark eyes, and the taste of fear. In the dark shadows around the edges of his dream lurked the evil Thing that had plagued him throughout his fast here.

He came fully awake, frightened and alert, wakened by his fear, and sat upright. It was a relief to be back in the real world, even in the dark of night. He looked around, and saw that there was a yellow-gray smudge at the horizon, the precursor of the dawn. He was glad.

Then he suddenly realized that his vision-quest was all but over. It should have been an enlightening experience, but it had raised more questions than it answered. Why, he asked himself? This was surely not how it was supposed to be. Again, he felt that something was interfering with his quest, leaving it unfinished.

Maybe he could talk to Looks Far, who might tell him the answers to some of his questions. Yes, and if that did not suffice, he supposed he could return . . . he was not certain if a person could attempt more than one vision-quest, but he must do something. This was definitely not finished.

He started to build up his fire as the dawn continued to lighten.

At least, he thought, he had managed to meet his spirit-guide. He smiled with satisfaction as he watched the flames grow.

He reached for his nearly empty water skin, took a sip to moisten his tongue, and smiled again.

"A *beaver!*" he murmured to himself.

# 6

>> >> >>

The sun rose, and White Fox performed the Morning Song once more. There was a strange mixture of feelings about this place. He was pleased and proud to have successfully carried out his vision-quest, and to have identified his spirit-guide. At the same time, he was reluctant to leave a place with so many unanswered questions. He did note, however, that with the coming of the sun the unknown had become a matter of curiosity rather than fear. Fear belonged to the darkness.

He smiled at himself for this reaction, and gathered up his few possessions, already planning the day. There was little to plan. He would return to the summer camp of his people. There he would, of course, stop at the lodge of his parents, and his mother would give him food. *Aiee,* it would be good to eat again!

One of his most important acts, however, would be to talk to Looks Far. He was eager to ask the medicine man for some of the answers he sought.

The camp was a day's journey away, and he must start, if he intended to be there by dark. He swung his robe across his shoulder, and started down the cliff path. He was about halfway down, when he noticed that the narrow trail branched, leading along the cliff's face in both directions. Odd, he had not noticed as he ascended. There was no question as to which was the correct way, and he moved on. A few steps later, curiosity caused him to turn and look again, to see why he had overlooked the other branch before.

Yes, it was obvious now. On his ascent of the cliff the first day, all his attention had been turned toward reaching the top. There had been no reason to look to the left as he climbed, for the trail obviously led on and up, the way he had gone before. He moved on, but then, curious, he turned back again, to look along the other pathway.

He could see for only a few steps before the path disappeared around a shoulder of the rock. It would do no harm, he decided, to take a quick look in that direction before he left.

Even as he stepped forward, it occurred to him that he had not realized the implications of the trail. He had made the mistake of assuming that this was a game trail, used only by animals. What sort of animal, he now asked himself, would inhabit the face of this cliff, moving along it frequently enough to wear such a path?

He remembered that in the mountains to the west, during the years the People traded with the Spanish there, his father had talked of such animals. Surely, though, there would be none here. And he had seen no droppings. The presence of deer, even, would have been easy to observe, from their little pellets of dung.

Now, as he moved along this trail, he began to have doubts as to the wisdom of even this brief look. He was again getting the strong feeling that he was not alone here, that he was watched. It was strong enough to make him pause and consider retreat. No, he decided, only one look around the shoulder of the rock.

He stepped around the projecting portion, to see only the trail, still clinging precariously to the rock's face as it crawled on ahead.

In some places it was dangerously narrow, but occasionally it broadened to a pace or two in width. There was such a place immediately ahead. Curiously, he glanced at the fringe of vegetation that clung to the crevices and cracks in the bluff's face along the trail.

Then he gasped and jumped back, almost falling over the edge as he did so. There, in plain sight on the wider portion of the shelf lay a corpse. It took a moment to overcome the fear that washed over him and made him doubt his own senses. Of all the things he might have encountered here, this was probably the most unexpected.

He regained his composure and resolved to consider what might have happened here, or what meaning it might have. The possibility occurred to him that he was still having visions from his fast, but he did not think so. No, this was real. He was strongly aware of the sickly smell of death now, and wondered that he had not observed it before.

The corpse was laid out full length, and wrapped in a buffalo robe. Beside the body lay a bow and arrows, and there were small packets that had undoubtedly contained food for the journey to the Other Side. It was all strikingly similar to the burial customs of the People. These amenities would have been carried out, and the body ceremonially placed on the burial scaffold with songs of mourning and with great honor to the dead.

Now another thought occurred to him that brought the prickle of fear again to the back of his neck. Who had carried out the ritual for this dead warrior? The dead man must be a warrior, or at least a hunter, because of the weapons. White Fox squatted on his heels to observe and try to understand this strange thing. The man had been tall, the length of the wrapped robe suggested. The general condition of the robe indicated that this death had occurred fairly recently, certainly no longer than a few moons ago. Possibly during the winter. The arrow points, he noted, were of flint, the blue-gray stone found in this area. This suggested that the dead man had had little contact with others, or he would have had at least one or two iron arrow points. His best, of course, would accompany him to the Other Side.

Could he have been a recluse, an outcast from the People or of another tribe, living here alone? Again, Fox was forced to reject this theory. It sometimes occurred that a person, alone and expecting death, would prepare himself for burial. One could set out food, weapons, perhaps dress for the journey and paint his face. Wrap himself in his robe, even, and cover his face. One thing he could not do, however. There was no way that the dying person could tie the thongs that fastened the robe around his arms, head, and neck. No, *someone* had carried out this ritual with respect and ceremony. But *who?*

As he pondered this mystery, White Fox was dimly aware of the sounds of the beaver family in the river below. There were playful splashes and the occasional slap of a tail on the water. Suddenly, however, there was a slap that was completely different. He had noted that there was a different quality in the slap of a genuine warning from the playful noises of fun. Now, this sound reverberated like the crack of a musket along the river, bouncing off the cliff and the trees. It was a truly authoritative warning. White Fox had only a moment to think of the figure of his vision, the beaver that was his spirit-guide. Even as he realized that the warning was for him, Fox started to rise, but was aware of the rush of an assailant behind him. He had only half turned when the full force of attack struck him. There was no time to reach for a weapon. He caught a glimpse of a stone knife in an upraised hand, and grasped frantically at that wrist.

The attacker was strong and wiry, and clawed, bit, kicked, and gouged as they struggled and rolled on the narrow ledge. Then they toppled over the edge, and there was the breathless sensation of falling. It was like a dream, where one's efforts are futile. He cannot run, or throw, or strike, only make a feeble effort. In this case, Fox was trying frantically to kick free, but was locked in the deadly embrace. The face was close to his, and in an instant he recognized the face that he had seen in his dreams, the unkempt long hair and the burning eyes, dark with terror. It could only have been the space of a few heartbeats that they fell, and then struck the surface of the water with a painful blow.

Still locked in combat, they plummeted deep. White Fox had managed to draw a last gasp of air to fill his lungs just before they struck the surface, but now he was frantic for breath. He did not know how much longer he could hold on before an involuntary gasp would fill his lungs with water. When it seemed that he could go no longer, suddenly his assailant's grasp weakened. Fox thrust the other from him, letting go the wrist that held the knife. Instantly the weapon thrust back at him, slashing his forearm through his buckskin shirt.

Frantically, he thrust away and swam toward the surface. Even as he did so, he realized that he would be attacked again. He reached for his knife, but it was gone. Then he caught a glimpse of a shadowy form in the water. A beaver, swimming strongly. With no real reason, except to escape the area of conflict, White Fox turned to follow the animal, his lungs still crying for air.

The river was narrow and deep at this point. He drew near the surface, leaving the dark of the water's depths below. Shimmering sunlight revealed that he had crossed the stream, and was approaching one of the stately old sycamores. The beaver swam straight ahead, toward a palisade of roots that reached from the bank and out into the water. White Fox followed.

He burst to the surface, gasping for air, behind the screen of knobby, knee-like sycamore roots, and turned to look back. The beaver had disappeared. He could see his attacker, floundering in the water along the other shore, searching for him. The other man suddenly turned, apparently attracted by the splashing as White Fox had surfaced. Now the dark eyes were looking directly at his hiding place.

White Fox could not have said why he reacted so, although later he realized that there was help from his spirit-guide. With his face still submerged nearly to the eyes, he extended a hand to arm's length, raised it, and slapped the water, firmly. The resulting crack, simulating the beaver's warning tail-slap, was enough. The assailant, now satisfied that the activity in the dim hollow under the sycamore was caused by beavers, turned away.

White Fox was able to relax a little now. He looked around for the beaver, but it was gone.

"Thank you, Grandfather," he murmured.

He turned to watch his assailant swimming and wading along the other shore, searching for any trace of the missing White Fox. Finally the man waded out of the water, his knife still in hand, to walk along the bank, peering into the water.

White Fox nearly gasped aloud. From beneath the other's buckskin tunic protruded long, shapely legs. The wet garment clung to a well-formed body, certainly not that of a man. His assailant was a woman! A girl, actually, no older than himself. She tossed her long hair back over her shoulder, and he now saw that the dark eyes were set in a face of remarkable beauty.

He had seen those eyes, in his dreams and visions, reflect a gamut of emotion. Fear, anger, terror, resentment, and determination. The determination he had seen not in a dream, however. It had been quite real. The girl had left no doubt in his mind. She had been determined to kill him.

# 7

### » » »

**W**hite Fox watched in astonishment as the girl paced up and down the bank, peering into the water. She moved with the lithe grace of a hunting cat, and it was with difficulty he realized that he, White Fox, was her intended prey. At the same time, he could not fail to appreciate the beauty of her face and form. She was the most attractive and stimulating woman he had ever seen. Perhaps the very danger in his present situation further stimulated his interest.

He remained still, peering out between the sycamore roots and trying not to attract the attention of the searcher. Certainly, her presence answered some of the questions that had plagued him during his vision-quest. Hers was the haunting face that had intruded in his visions. She was undoubtedly responsible for the feeling of interference that had become so definite a thing. She may have been the person who had ceremoniously wrapped the corpse on the ledge above. Certainly, she had something to do with the

dead warrior. She had possibly attacked because of his interest in
the corpse.

The girl's presence raised more doubts than it answered, however. Who could she be? Why did she seem to inhabit this place of
the spirits? Was it possible that she herself was a supernatural
being? No, he thought not. Her attack was quite skilled and human, and his wound had been inflicted by a flint knife that was far
from supernatural.

But maybe . . . there was the recurrent theme in his visions of
something dreadful and incredibly evil. Maybe it was she herself,
deceptively playing with his mind, pretending to be human, so
that his spirit would be lulled off guard, softened for the attack of
the evil Thing that had inhabited his dream.

Another chilling thought occurred to him. The old tales, told
around the story fires, were full of beings who could change form
at will. Could not the evil Thing change, to appear to him as a
beautiful woman? Such deception would be a simple thing for a
supernatural being such as the evil Thing of his dreams.

Now he was thoroughly confused. He felt fear of the woman
who had tried to kill him, but it was a reasonable fear. It was not
like the stark terror that had stalked him in the darkness. He could
not have explained the difference, but it was there. Could it be the
difference in form, when the evil Thing changed to become human?

No matter, he thought. He would soon be away from this intense place and its powerful spirits. It had been a mistake to
choose such a place for his vision-quest. He would talk with Looks
Far and maybe that would help to clear his confused thoughts.
Something must, or he would surely go mad.

Now, the girl had apparently decided that her victim was dead,
somewhere in the depths of the river's dark pools. He could sense
in the resigned shrug of her shoulders that her search was over. She
sheathed her knife, turned, and started up the face of the cliff. Fox
was impressed by the fact that there must be several paths and
means of ascent. The ease with which this girl climbed the rock

suggested that she knew every foothold and projection, from long acquaintance. Her movements seemed effortless, without deliberation. He thought in passing of the lithe grace of a squirrel, and its ability to scamper among branches high above the ground. This girl showed such a confidence in her climb.

Then she was gone. She vanished so suddenly that the thought crossed his mind that she had transformed herself . . . no, that was ridiculous. If she had the ability to transform herself, she would have become a bird and *flown* up, rather than climb.

He shook his head to clear it. Maybe he was already going mad. He must get away from here.

He slipped under the water, between the sycamore roots, and swam downstream underwater. He headed for the concealment of a growth of willows that would screen him from observation by searching eyes on the rock. He was completely without weapons, having lost his bow on the burial ledge, and his knife during the plunge to the river. He had been fortunate, actually. The fall could easily have killed him. Then the assistance of his spirit-guide, who had warned him of the attack and then shown him the way to escape. *Aiee*, it was good to have such a guide!

Cautiously, he emerged from the stream, looking across to the cliff for any sign of pursuit. There was none. Now, he must move quickly. He had been longer than he intended at the rock, and the sun was high. It would require sustained travel to reach home by dark. Maybe that did not matter so much now, he thought. He could travel after dark. It would be in familiar territory and nearing home.

Even as he thought, he was moving. He settled into an easy jogging wolf-trot that covered distance without tiring. Occasionally he slowed to a walk for a while to rest his muscles. When Sun Boy was directly overhead, he stopped and lay full length on the grass. He would have eaten, but he had nothing. He would not break his fast until evening, but he was increasingly feeling the need to reach home and talk to Looks Far.

There were many things he did not understand. Increasingly, he was becoming aware that he was fortunate to be alive. He had even successfully completed his vision-quest. At least, he thought he had. There was much about it that did not seem appropriate, but . . . ah, well, Looks Far could tell him.

Then there was the girl with the large dark eyes and the beautiful body. He had felt strongly attracted to her. Yet, he told himself ruefully, she had tried to kill him. He examined the gash on his forearm. It had stopped bleeding without difficulty, after he had applied pressure. The cut was a hand's span in length, but appeared not to be too deep. It would heal. He pressed the skin edges together, but could not keep them so. He had no way to bind the wound, no knife to cut strips from his shirt or leggings.

A fly buzzed near, investigating the fresh blood. White Fox shooed it away, and rose to his feet. It was time to move on, and while he was moving, the flies would be less bother to his injured arm. When he reached home, he could dress the wound.

And eat. He wondered if his thoughts would be affected by a return to food, and if so, how? Looks Far would know, of course, but he would not ask him that. There were much more important things to speak of.

Distance continued to slide beneath Fox's feet as Sun Boy continued his daily run down the western slope of the sky. Yes, White Fox estimated now, he should reach the village at just about dark.

# 8

≫ ≫ ≫

"**T**ell me only if you wish," cautioned Looks Far.

White Fox thought for a moment.

"Is it proper to tell of my quest?"

"Yes, of course. Many do not speak of the experience, because it is so private a thing, but there is no law forbidding it."

"It is good," said Fox with some degree of relief. "Uncle, I *must* talk of this."

It was fully dark, and the two were walking under dim starlight, to be a little away from the noise and confusion of the camp. They came to the crest of a little hill and looked down on the scattered lodges below. White Fox felt the comfortable familiarity of the band's summer camp, and it was good to be home. The points of light below marked outside cooking fires. The People cooked in the lodges only in winter or in bad weather.

He had arrived at the lodge of his parents just before nightfall. Moonflower embraced him and hastened to set food before him.

"What happened to your arm?" she asked anxiously.

"An accident," Fox shrugged. "It is nothing."

"Here, I will wrap it," his mother insisted.

She drew out strips of cloth and dressed the injury, rubbing it gently with an ointment she took from a small gourd. Fox continued to eat.

Yes, he told his father, it was a successful vision-quest. He did not go into great detail, wishing to discuss the matter with the medicine man first. Red Feather was well aware of the privacy of the vision-quest, and did not press him. Both parents understood his urgent need to talk to Looks Far.

"Go on," Red Feather encouraged, as Fox finished his food. "We will talk later."

White Fox tapped on the lodge cover to announce his presence.

"Looks Far?" he called, "it is White Fox, back from the vision-quest. May we talk, Uncle?"

*"Aiee*, it is good!" called the old medicine man. "I will come out."

He stooped and emerged from the lodge, and the door-skin fell back into place.

"Let us walk," Looks Far had suggested.

Now, in the quiet of the prairie, they sat down to begin their talk in earnest. White Fox felt that the older man was as eager as he, but the indifferent reserve of age and experience held fast.

Both men were quiet for a little while. White Fox listened to the guttural cry of a night heron in the willows along the stream. It was a reassuring sound.

"Uncle," he said finally, "there is much that I do not understand."

Looks Far nodded.

"There is much that I do not understand, also," he agreed.

"No, no, Uncle. It is not that. The vision-quest. I am not sure it was as it should be."

"It is different for each," observed Looks Far. "But what is your doubt? You found no spirit-guide?"

"Oh, yes, I did," White Fox answered eagerly. "Already, he has saved me once."

Even in the dim starlight, Fox could see the wide-eyed look of amazement on the old medicine man's face. However, he said nothing.

White Fox did not know where to begin. There were so many questions. Finally he held out his injured arm.

"An accident?" Looks Far asked, unimpressed.

"No, someone tried to kill me."

Now the composure of Looks Far was shattered.

"*Aiee,*" he exclaimed. "Someone else was there? Your spirit-guide came anyway?"

"This is one of my questions, Uncle," White Fox said, almost desperately. "If someone else was at the Medicine Rock, are my visions good?"

"If your spirit-guide came, yes," Looks Far said thoughtfully. "It must be powerful, to break through such interference."

"But I did not know until later, Uncle. I . . ."

"Wait!" Looks Far held up a hand. "Maybe you better start at the beginning. Now, tell me only what you wish; leave out anything you need to."

White Fox nodded and his story came pouring forth, beginning with his arrival and the climb to the top of the rock. When he came to the description of the fear he had experienced in his dream-visions, Looks Far held up a hand.

"Wait," he said. "You feared *what?*"

"I do not know, Uncle. That is part of the question. It was like some evil, some *Thing* that threatened. Is this part of the quest?"

Looks Far pondered a moment.

"I think not," he said slowly. "It may be the interference from someone else's presence. But go on. You did not come to that yet."

White Fox related how his spirit had seemed to become one with those of the creatures around him, describing the feeling of flight, the herd feeling of the buffalo, and the timid spirit of the mouse in the grass clump.

Looks Far nodded, pleased. Fox described his meeting with Grandfather Beaver, and his pleasure in it, and the old man was pleased again.

When he told of his feeling that he was not alone, Looks Far stopped him.

"Yes, this was the other person. My son, yours must be powerful medicine, to succeed in spite of this!"

"But wait, Uncle. I have not told all!"

When he came to the part about the corpse, Looks Far gasped aloud. By the time the spirit-guide had warned him, and Fox and the attacker had gone over the cliff, the medicine man was staring, open-mouthed. The final shock, that the assailant was a woman, seemed to render him speechless.

The old man sat silent for a long time, and White Fox waited. Finally, Looks Far took a deep breath and spoke, softly and slowly.

"My son, there is much here that I do not understand. It is strange that you are even alive. Your medicine must be very powerful. Now, we have two things here to think of. There is your vision-quest, which was good, with a strong spirit-guide. The other, the stranger . . . this has nothing to do with the vision-quest. It might have happened anyway."

He paused again, deep in thought.

"Look," he went on, "maybe a young couple was staying at the rock, and he died, or was killed. His wife would prepare the body, and then maybe stay to mourn."

"But, Uncle, the body has been there several moons!"

"I do not know, Fox. Maybe she is a little crazy. She did try to kill you. You say she was young?"

"Yes, and beautiful. Except, her hair was not properly cared for."

"See? A young wife in mourning!"

"Why would she try to kill me?"

"Maybe . . . look, you were near the bones of her husband! She feared you would disturb him, and resented your presence."

This explanation seemed plausible, and more likely as they discussed it further.

"Well, it is no matter now," Looks Far finally concluded, rising. "Your quest is over, you are safe; your Woman-of-the-Rock will go back to her people when she is ready. It is good to have you home, my son. Now, let us go and take our rest!"

They headed back toward the camp, where the scattered cooking fires were dying to an occasional dark red ember. White Fox felt greatly relieved. It was good to have the reassurance of the medicine man.

Now, suddenly, he was tired, and wanted only to seek his sleeping robes. *Aiee*, it was good to be home.

# 9

**》》 》》 》》**

He could see just a small patch of starry night sky as he lay on his sleeping-robes. It was a warm night, and he had untied the thongs and rolled the lodge skin up to allow a bit of south breeze to come through. That made the night more comfortable, but did not help him sleep. He lay there wide-eyed and stared at the patch of stars as they circled slowly past the opening in their nightly journey around the Real-star.

He had thought he would be sleepy, exhausted from his hard journey. Instead, excitement kept him awake and alert. He relived every thrilling moment of his vision-quest, every reassuring word of the medicine man. He thought again of his dreams, and the simple explanation, once he had shared his questions with Looks Far.

It was good. Now, with the joyous discoveries of his vision-quest, and the identification of his spirit-guide, he could settle down to a more normal life than the last few years had afforded. It was probably time for him to find a wife and establish their own lodge. He wondered if the spirit-guide would assist in that, too. It would certainly be a major change in his life. He hoped that his wife would be as beautiful as the girl who had tried to kill him.

What an odd thought! Disturbed by its bizarre implications, he rolled over, now facing into the dark interior of the lodge. He could hear the deep breathing of his parents in their bed of robes opposite the lodge door.

He tried to reject the sensual desirability of the girl at the Rock, but she kept intruding into his thoughts. She had appeared so unconscious of her beauty, yet her every motion had demonstrated it. Ah, well, there was no harm in wishing that the one who would consent to be his wife could look like that.

Now that Looks Far had helped him to understand the probable reasons for the girl's presence there, he found that he had a great deal of sympathy for her. Ah, what tragedy! Perhaps, even, she and her new husband had been on their marriage quest when tragedy had struck. *Aiee,* how difficult for her. She had carefully wrapped the body, and mourned his passing, and then . . . but why had she stayed? Surely, in the ensuing moons, she would have returned to her people, or they would have come looking for her. Maybe it was as Looks Far suggested, she was a little bit crazy. Maybe she was crazy *before* the death of her husband.

Another thought startled him, and he rolled over to look questioningly at the stars again. Maybe she was crazy, and had *killed* her husband, as she had tried to kill White Fox. A cold chill crept between his shoulder blades and up his neck. What if the corpse was that of a vision-seeker like himself, who had been killed by the crazed recluse. It was a possibility, a very real one. If true, it strongly suggested that White Fox had narrowly escaped becoming a second corpse in a burial robe, decaying on a ledge at Medicine Rock.

Were there others? He had seen strong evidence that there might be a network of paths on the cliff's face. Were other ledges adorned with other rotting corpses? He shuddered. The thought came to him that this woman might be like the large black and yellow spider which spun its intricate webs each fall. Insects flying past would blunder into the trap. He had watched the spider catch creatures as big as a large grasshopper. As soon as the prey struck the web, the spider would run and pounce on the struggling creature, wrapping it tightly . . . wrapping it like a corpse for burial! How odd that he had not seen the similarity before.

A little earlier he had felt reassured and well informed. Now he feared that his talk with Looks Far had sent him off in an entirely wrong direction. The explanation proposed by Looks Far, for instance, did not even begin to answer his impression that there was some evil Thing at Medicine Rock. In their desire to understand, both he and the medicine man had overlooked that fact. White Fox had had the definite sense of fear, repeatedly, while he was there. Of terror, almost. Terror of the evil inhabitant of the Rock.

Following this new line of thought, were the murderous girl and the creature of evil the *same?* Was *she* the evil Thing? Did she decoy men there, entrap them with her beauty, and kill them to place them on the rock? Was she, after all, a supernatural creature, changing from a terrible death-dealing creature to a beautiful woman? He wondered again about the crevice filled with bones. Was he *certain* that those were animal bones?

No, he decided. It was clearly the woman who had attacked him. If a supernatural being with power to transform had wished to attack, it would do so in the form of a bear or a wolf or a warrior, not as a woman with a small flint knife. So, if the woman was of flesh and blood, she could still be crazy. She could still be a killer.

This, however, did not explain his terror of the evil Thing, and that idea kept coming back. He tried to think of when he first felt it. When he started down the trail a little way, on that first day, to get more firewood? No, he had felt that someone else was present, but not the fear. The presence could have been that of the girl, but the evil seemed to be something else. Puzzled, he thought further. He had felt the ability, after the effects of fasting, to leave the fetters of his body, and enter the minds of the creatures around him. He had been one with the hawk, the mouse, the dark fish in the stream, the buffalo. And, of course, the girl. He was just now beginning to understand that he had been inside her head, too. That had not been apparent to him, because he did not know of her existence at the time. He had felt only her hatred and fear. And his own fear, of course.

But wait, he thought. In that vision-state, he would not know what to fear, except the fear of those spirits which touched his own. That was why he had had so much trouble understanding his terror, and in trying to identify the evil Thing. The unspeakably evil creature whose nature he could not quite grasp was not the girl at all!

He sat up in his robes, now understanding more, but more deeply concerned than ever. The first time that he had felt the evil had been when his spirit first encountered the girl's. But since he had been "inside her head," the fear and terror that he felt were not his own. He had misunderstood. Not knowing what to expect, he thought he was feeling terror and the presence of evil. Instead, he only now realized, he had been feeling the girl's terror, and the creature of evil, the unspeakable Thing, was a part of *her* fears. It was exactly the same as when he felt the timid fear of the mouse in the grass.

Of course! Now, even Looks Far's theory was appropriate. The girl, left alone by the death of her husband, had been living in terror of some evil being ever since. His sympathy for her returned. In her loneliness and bereavement, the poor girl had created the evil in her own mind, and it was now ruling her. Yes, she was undoubtedly a little crazy, and her madness was creating the evil something that had terrorized White Fox when he entered her mind under the state of his vision-fast.

Fox lay back down and rolled under the raised lodge cover, to stand up outside. There was no sleeping now. He did not know whether he could wait until morning to approach Looks Far. Looking to the east, he saw a gray smudge on the horizon that heralded the false dawn. He threaded his way among the lodges of the sleeping village until he reached that of the medicine man. There he squatted on his heels to wait.

It seemed a long time before the door skin lifted and Looks Far came out into the graying darkness, stretching and yawning. He started around toward the back of the lodge to urinate, but White Fox called to him.

"*Aiee,*" said Looks Far sleepily. "You again? What is it now?"

"Uncle," Fox began, "we talked of the girl at Medicine Rock."

"Yes, but . . ."

"We also talked of my fear of something evil, some Thing?"

"Yes, Fox. But that was when you did not know of the girl. Look, my bladder calls. I will be back."

The old man hurried around the lodge, but soon returned.

"Ah, yes, that is better. Now, what have you thought?"

"Only this, Uncle. My fear of the evil was when I did not know I was in the girl's head. It was *her* fear."

Looks Far's eyes widened.

"Yes, I am made to believe you are right," he said slowly. "And now?"

"Well, if it is her fear, is it real, or is she crazy? Or am I?"

Now, Looks Far waited a long time before he answered, and then it was with a question.

"You felt an evil *something?*"

"Yes, but it was her fear."

"True. My son, first, I do not think you are crazy. The girl may be, but . . ."

"But is the evil Thing real, or only in her head?"

"It does not matter," Looks Far said seriously. "Only whether *she* thinks it real. And she does, it seems, from the way you felt her fears. Fox, this woman is in great danger."

White Fox had come to this conclusion already. He could understand the terror in which the girl lived, because he had felt it.

"Uncle," he said slowly, and with a great deal of reluctance, "I must go back to the Rock."

Looks Far nodded.

"I will help you."

"No, I must go alone."

"Of course," the medicine man agreed, "but I will teach you some things that may help you. One should not go into battle unarmed."

# 10
>> >> >>

**H**e crouched behind a fringe of sumac and peered toward the cliff across the river. He could see no sign of the girl, but he knew she was there, and he must be careful not to show himself. He would use today to observe, see if he could determine the girl's routine, and choose a strategic place to conceal himself before the sun rose again.

White Fox and Looks Far had talked long and earnestly about the problems involved in returning to the Rock. Although Looks Far wished to help in any possible way, there were some things that both agreed he would be unable to do. Specifically, it seemed unwise for him to become directly involved. He could not accompany White Fox back to Medicine Rock.

"It is a matter of your own medicine," Looks Far explained. "I will help you, but I cannot go."

They spent that morning in instruction, with Looks Far attempting to share his knowledge of the chants and ceremonial dances. At times, he became frustrated.

"No, no! Not that way! It goes like this!"

Painstakingly he would go over the intricacies of the ceremony again.

"You know," he reminded White Fox, "it might take years to learn this. *Aiee,* I would not even try, but your medicine has proved so strong. And, it is very important."

Unspoken, but plain to both, was the implication that the instruction involved might become a matter of life and death, both for White Fox and for the mysterious girl. Looks Far assisted in the preparation of a medicine pouch for the young man. There were some things that it must contain. A pinch of fur from the beaver, his medicine animal. For the same reason, a few drops of musk from the scent glands of the same creature. The musk was placed in a vial made from the hollow wing bone of an eagle, and carefully stoppered with a wooden plug.

"These things are only a start," Looks Far warned. "You must add to your medicine for the rest of your life."

He also furnished an assortment of powdered and shredded plant materials, with carefully memorized instructions.

"We do not have time for you to learn it all," the old man cried in frustration. "Just remember what I tell you! *Aiee,* you may not have a chance to use it at all!"

By the time White Fox was ready to depart, the old medicine man was calmer and more philosophical.

"Remember, my son," he cautioned, "there is no single answer to this. Nor to anything, maybe. You must think, plan, but be ready to change, to do what is right at the time."

"And how will I know, Uncle?"

"You will not," Looks Far cautioned. "Nothing is ever just as we thought it would be, so we do what we must!"

This advice was little comfort to White Fox as he crouched in the sumac thicket and watched the cliff. He could see more and more problems, and fewer and fewer solutions.

They had planned his departure and travel so that he would arrive at night, well before dawn's light would reveal his presence.

This had allowed him to conceal himself, to observe unseen for the day. He had doubts about the whole mission. The thought had occurred to him as he lay waiting for dawn that the girl might have different habits than normal humans. Maybe she prowled and hunted during the night, like the owl or the bobcat, and spent her days sleeping, except when disturbed, as he had done. Maybe, in the darkness before the dawn, she was watching him, able to see in the dark, like the other creatures of the night. She could be creeping up to attack even now . . .

It was a very uncomfortable feeling, which became only a little more tolerable after sunrise. By that time he had spent some time with another thought that was quite disturbing: were there *others* living on the Rock, or in its caves and crevices? There had been at least the one, whose body lay rotting on the ledge over beyond the sycamore.

No, he must reject the confusing influence of such ideas. He must continue to think what his senses and his visions all indicated. This was a completely human girl. She was alone, or his vision-quest would have allowed him to feel another presence. He had felt none, except for the undefined threat of terror which he now believed he had felt through the girl's spirit. He, and Looks Far as well, also believed the girl to be in great danger.

So, he would now watch, and plan his opportunity. He was far from certain what he intended to do. It would be logical to try to talk to the girl, but there were problems in that, too. He was completely uncertain how she would react. It was difficult to overlook the fact that at their first meeting she had tried to kill him. It had been an effective try, and only the intervention of his spirit-guide had saved him.

Even at best, if she did not make another attempt on his life, the girl might run. Then, forewarned of his presence, she could make contact virtually impossible. She knew these surroundings, and White Fox did not. She could elude him forever. Or, until whatever caused her terror had worked its evil purpose.

No, he must go slowly. As Looks Far had pointed out, he must be prepared to change his approach at any moment. "Nothing is ever just as we thought it would be . . ." First, he must locate the girl and see where she lived, ate, and drank. Then who knows, he thought. Something would occur that would help him to plan his next move. He would proceed cautiously, waiting until he had more information.

This was much like hunting, it occurred to him. Not in the great buffalo hunts, where mounted riders engaged in a chase into the herd. But sometimes when game was scarce, it became important to know the old ways. It might be necessary to lie unmoving for long periods of time, maybe day after day, to watch the habits of the intended quarry. Only in this way could the hunter manage to be in the right place at the right time for one all-important single shot that would provide food. It might not be at the time and place he expected, but without knowledge of the quarry's habits there would be no chance at all.

The sun had hardly begun to climb when there was a flash of motion on the face of the cliff opposite White Fox's position. Quickly, he focused his gaze on that spot. It was about three-fourths of the way to the top of the rock, and a long bow shot from the sumac where he lay. The girl had emerged from some hiding place in the rock, and now paused, partially hidden from his view by a large boulder on the ledge. It was apparent that her purpose was to search for any possible danger.

White Fox lay perfectly still while the girl stared for what seemed a very long time. An ant crawled along his moccasin, over its top and up his bare leg for a little distance. The tickling sensation was almost unbearable. No sooner had the ant moved on than a fly chose to alight on Fox's nose, walking inquisitively across his forehead, down the cheek, and onto his lip. At this point he managed to assume a facial expression that required enough motion to alarm the insect, and it moved on.

Finally the girl seemed reassured and rose to move along the path. While she was motionless, she had seemed virtually invisible. Her hair, shoulders, and the ragged skins she wore seemed to blend with the boulder and the rough face of the cliff to form a colorless oneness. For a few moments, Fox even thought that she had vanished before his eyes. Then she moved, and he watched her stop along the cliff's face, slanting downward toward the river.

Once she paused and studied the terrain again for a long time. She seemed to look directly at him, and he thought that he had been seen. Then her eyes swept on, and he relaxed. She paused once again for a little while, and he could not see what she was doing. He thought that it may have been at the ledge where the burial-wrapped body lay, but he could not be certain. The different perspective made it difficult to estimate.

She made her way on down to the shore and stopped again for one more long, deliberate look. She carried a bow and arrows, and Fox was well aware of the little knife that rested in the sheath at her waist.

Now she laid aside the bow, loosened the thong around her waist, and lifted the nondescript skin garment over her head. She tossed it to the grass beside the bow and stepped into the water.

White Fox had been hypnotized by her beauty on their previous encounter, even wounded and hiding for his life. He had been closer then, hiding under the sycamore, but now, even at a greater distance, the viewing of her body totally naked was a powerful shock. It should not have been, really. That she would come down to the river to bathe was as natural as the coming of day, and should have been no surprise.

The girl waded into the water until it reached her knees. Then she plunged forward, head first, into the depths of the channel. She swam underwater for a little way, and then surfaced, playfully splashing, swimming powerfully for a few strokes, diving again. She was an excellent swimmer. White Fox realized even more surely that he was fortunate to have survived the attack and the struggle in the water. He wondered if the girl believed that she had killed him in the river. Certainly, she seemed unconcerned now, completely confident.

Finally she waded ashore, stripping water from her skin with her hands, and squeezing it from her long hair. Once more, the provocative sensuality that he had seen before excited him. Her every motion was lithe and graceful, and it was difficult to keep his mind on his purpose here.

She picked up the tunic she had dropped on the grass, and slid it over her head. She grasped her hair, still shining wet, to pull it free, squeezing it dry as she handled it. Then she shook it over her shoulder with a toss that could only have been described as proud. She wrapped the thong around her waist, settled the knife in its sheath, and slipped into her moccasins. Then she picked up her bow and arrows, and crossed the river at the riffle. For a moment, White Fox feared that she was moving in his direction, but she turned to go upstream.

From every appearance, she was off on a morning hunt. She disappeared in the trees, and White Fox began to breathe a little easier.

But who could she *be?*

# 11

>> >> >>

It was midday when White Fox became alert to the return of the girl. The day was warm, and the thin, mottled shade of the sumac was quite inadequate for relief from the heat of Sun Boy's torch. Fox had tried to wriggle into a more shaded position without too much apparent movement, but his ability to do so was limited. He disturbed a small bird whose nest was nearby, and the scolding that this precipitated quickly became a threat. He considered moving his position, but was afraid that he would be seen by the returning woman. That would eliminate his entire effort so far.

He compromised by lying very still and trying to ignore the repeated scolding chirps of alarm from the disturbed bird. It would eventually stop, he knew. Hopefully, before it attracted unwanted attention.

"Go back to your lodge, mother," he thought, trying to project the idea to the frantic bird. "I mean no harm."

After what seemed a long time, the bird's alarm began to subside. She came closer, and when no motion resulted, seemed to decide that the fearsome creature in the grass presented no threat. She alighted on the nest, turned a time or two to roll the eggs to new positions, and settled down to the task of incubation.

Another threat, less to his safety but greater to his bodily comfort, was that of insects. Mosquitoes were numerous under the screen of the sumac thicket, and he was constantly under attack. From time to time, a deerfly would alight unseen on an ankle or other exposed portion of skin. His first inkling of its presence would be a sharp jab of pain from the bite. He reflected glumly that if this vigil had been a few days later, the problem would be lessened. The eggs of the small brown bird in the nest in front of him would have hatched. Hungry nestlings would require tremendous quantities of food. Both parents would be hunting and catching large numbers of the very insects that were now chewing his exposed skin into a mass of swollen lumps.

His first inkling of the girl's return was the alarm call of a blue jay in the trees along the stream. He glanced in that direction. He had chosen his position so that he could do so without moving. At first, he saw nothing. Then a deer moved into sight, not really alarmed, but moving out of the way of danger. Something was coming.

He did not actually see the girl at first. One moment she was not there, and the next she had suddenly appeared. She was standing, partially behind the trunk of a sycamore, and looking downstream to locate any danger, before coming into the open. Fox did not know how he could have failed to see her appear there, before his very eyes. In the mottled shade, which flickered and shifted with the breeze, she was still almost invisible.

There was the distant slap of a beaver's tail, and he wondered if his spirit-guide was at work. How would he know whether it was merely any beaver . . .

"Thank you, Grandfather. I see her," he thought silently.

It would do no harm to assume that his medicine was good. It was not important, actually, only that the warning *did* come to him.

Now the girl was stepping into the open, moving cautiously, glancing suspiciously from side to side. A fat young rabbit hung from her waist, indicating a successful hunt. Once more White Fox was impressed by her beauty. Long, well-formed legs carried her in a few strides across the open space to the gravel bar and across the riffle to the other shore. There she turned to look at her back trail. There was an instant when the haunting dark eyes of his dream seemed to look directly at him, and he tried to be invisible.

Then the girl stooped gracefully and drank from a cupped hand, watching all the while. She rose, turned, and started up the path to the cliff. In the area where he had first observed her in the morning, she suddenly seemed to vanish into some unseen crevice. She did not reappear.

Ah, he thought, that is her lodge! He watched closely, and after a time he thought he saw a wisp of white smoke from the same part of the cliff. Then it was gone, but a little later the light breeze, shifting along the river and the cliff face, brought a whiff of pungent smoke to his nostrils. Then it, too, was gone, and there seemed to be no trace of the cooking fire that he knew was necessary. The girl was very skillful, it appeared. Not only was she able to select practically smokeless fuel, but to choose the best time of day for her cooking fire. In the evening, and even for a while in the mornings, the scent of smoke would be flowing down the cliff's face with the cooling air. Anyone who chanced to be along the river for some distance could possibly scent the smoke. Now, with the midday sun warming the cliff's face, any scent would be carried high aloft on the same rising air that allowed the hawk to soar. It would rapidly diffuse in the wide prairie sky, avoiding detection.

Now White Fox turned his attention to selecting his next hiding place. It seemed that the girl would probably repeat her daily routine as a usual thing. There was a thicket of dogwood at the base of the rock, where her trail emerged from the crevice. He could hide there, and when she came down the trail the next morning . . .

He considered stepping out to confront her, but again, rejected that approach. She would either attack him, or turn and flee, back up the cliff. There she would be at an advantage, because she would know the terrain. No, he must be in control of the situation. It would be necessary to capture her, probably to tie her, to obtain any chance to communicate.

As he considered the area, the thicket seemed to be the likeliest spot to conceal himself. It faced on a grassy strip next to the water. The strip was level, smooth, and no more than three or four paces wide. There was room for the brief scuffle in which he would subdue his quarry and tie her.

Then he would have the task of communication. He did not know what tongue she might understand. In the few times he had seen her, there was no clue as to her tribe. Her weapons could be characteristic of any tribe in the area. The loose tunic of skins which covered her from neck to midthigh, however, belonged to no group he had ever encountered. The garment was made of skins tanned with the fur on, not a usual custom. Among the People and their allies, it would be more usual to use soft-tanned buckskin, and then for warmth in inclement weather, add a buffalo robe. Well, soon he would find out.

He waited until well after dark, when all was quiet and the creatures of the night had begun their usual songs. Mosquitoes were becoming even more numerous, and he did not believe he could last much longer in his present position. There was no sign of activity on the cliff face now, and he cautiously rose to his feet. The stiffness in his muscles sent jabs of pain through his legs, and for a moment, he found it difficult to stand. Then he gathered his medicine bag and his weapons, tossed his robe over a shoulder, and moved down the slope toward the river.

He was careful to keep the branches of a big cottonwood between him and that critical portion of the cliff where he presumed the girl's lodge to be. He paused frequently to listen for any change in the song of the night creatures, but there was none. The deep-voiced frog sounded his call from the cattails, echoed by the hunting owl. Upstream the beavers were at play.

Fox stepped to the head of the gravel bar and paused to look at the cliff's face once more. There was no sign of life, and he nodded in satisfaction as he moved on across the river. He stopped on the other side and knelt to drink, then cupped water in both hands to soothe his swollen face. Somewhat relieved, he turned to consider his selected hiding place at close hand.

The thicket appeared to be a good choice. It was not dense, but would provide the concealment that he needed. He moved along, searching for the best place to enter. The light was none too good, only the dim starlight in the darkness of the waning phase of the moon. There would be some light later, but it would be some time before moonrise. He had planned to avoid discovery by being well hidden long before that time. His problem, of course, was that while the darkness concealed his movements, it also hindered his own ability to see.

He peered between the dogwood stems, the thickness of his thumb and taller than his head. The blooms were nearly gone, and he thought for a moment how rapidly the summer was passing. He selected a hiding place and stooped to pass under the overhanging branch of the outermost shrub.

It was then that several things seemed to happen at once. There was the sound of a beaver's warning slap from behind him. Before he could react from his surprise, he was aware of a rush from his right. He straightened and started to turn to face the attack, realizing as he did so that he had not reacted well to his spirit-guide's warning. There was no time to raise a hand in his own defense before the attack struck. He had only a momentary glimpse of haunting dark eyes filled with rage, before something struck his head. Then even the dim starlight turned to absolute blackness, like a buffalo robe thrown over all the world.

# 12

**»» »» »»**

He opened his eyes to total darkness, and at first assumed that he must be dead. A frightening thought occurred to him. The Head Splitters, allies of the People, had always hesitated to fight at night. They believed that a spirit separating from the body in the night would lose its way, and be doomed to wander in darkness forever. He now recalled this belief with some degree of panic. *Aiee,* were the Head Splitters right all along? This impenetrable blackness . . . *forever?*

He tried to turn his head to see any signs of light. This was reassuring. In his confused state he had not stopped to consider whether a spirit might even be able to think in terms of turning its head. Now he found that the muscles of his neck and shoulders did, indeed, still function. That was reassuring. It was also quite painful. A dull ache that he had hardly recognized as a part of him now settled in with a vengeance. It became a throbbing, pounding pain that began at the base of his skull and progressed forward to

settle behind his eyes. Or began behind his eyes to progress back
. . . *aiee*, it did not matter. It even hurt to blink his eyes. This
verified his impression that he must be alive. If he were dead, he
could feel no pain.

He tried to raise a hand to his throbbing head, and discovered
that his hands were tightly tied. His feet, also, he now realized.
There was numbness through his entire body, stiffness from lying
in one position. Now he also began to realize some other physical
sensations. He was lying on a soft-furred robe. A buffalo robe,
maybe. He tried to think. The Rock, the girl . . . he had been
trying to find a hiding place from which to . . . *aiee*, the girl had
beaten him at his own game! He must now be her prisoner. At
least, someone's prisoner. This was an alarming situation, but at
least he was alive. The girl, if it was she who had captured him,
had spared his life. That was a great step forward, considering that
at their last encounter she had tried to kill him.

He attempted to discover more about his surroundings. It was
warm but not uncomfortably so, and there was no breeze. His nose
also told him that this was a place of habitation. There were warm
animal smells, and the unmistakable scents of smoke and tanned
animal skins. It must be a lodge of some sort, like those built partly
into the ground, such as the Growers use. But . . . no, of course!
This must be a cave in the cliff. He had suspected that the girl's
dwelling must be something like this. The bump on the head must
be affecting his thinking.

Now another question occurred to him. Was the girl here in the
darkness with him? He held his breath to gain absolute silence, and
listened for the breathing of another person. There was nothing.
She had apparently left the cave again. This did nothing to reassure him. He thought again of his idea that maybe she could see in
the dark.

That brought on another alarming question. For what purpose
had she captured him? And again there came the bizarre thoughts
of the spider, attracting insects to its web. The corpse on the
ledge. Was her purpose to torture and kill? For a moment panic

gripped him, and he struggled against the thongs on his wrists. It was useless, and he forced himself to relax. He must try to discover more about his surroundings.

He was lying on his side, and as he moved a little he discovered that his back was against a solid wall of stone. This, then, would be one wall of the dwelling. He could now begin to visualize in his mind the rest of the cave. There would be a fire . . . yes, there was a definite sensation of warmth from an area about two paces from his head. The coals would be covered with ash, so nothing would show at this time.

Which way would the entrance be? He was still straining his eyes to determine any area where there seemed to be less density to the darkness when he heard the noise. Soft footsteps to his left, closer with each step. It was still only a quiet rustle of leather on stone, but it was there. He felt a presence enter the cave, and a hint of the smell of night air. The girl had been outside.

She came straight toward him, and Fox tried desperately to feign sleep. He felt her hands on him, quick and deliberate, yet gentle. She felt the thongs on his wrists and ankles, leaning across him to investigate the bandage on his forearm from their previous encounter. He felt the closeness of her body, the warm woman smell of her, and remembered the exquisite appearance of that body at the stream. What was he thinking of, he demanded angrily of himself. This woman might soon torture and kill him. The emotion of the moment interrupted the regular rhythm of his breathing, and the girl tensed. Her hands moved to his head, gently touching his face, then moving to the back of his head. He now realized that a tender area there indicated the site of the blow. He wondered what she had used to strike him.

Through all of this, he had tried to resume the regular breathing of a sleeper, or of one unconscious. He did not know whether he was successful or not. There was a guttural sound from the girl's throat as she turned away. It may have been a remark to herself in a tongue he did not understand, but it sounded more like an animal's growl or grunt.

That made him think once more of the question as to whether she might indeed be a supernatural being. Could he have been present at a moment when she transformed herself to a wolf, a bear, or a great cat? It was a terrifying thought. He heard her lie down, hardly a pace away from him. She seemed to settle herself (like a cat?) and then at once he heard the deep regular breathing of sleep.

There would be no sleep for White Fox. Any or all of his thoughts about this situation were so terrifying that it would be easy to panic, and he fought that down. At least, he was alive. He was uninjured, except for the aching head. The girl could easily have killed him, but had not. That, at least, should count for something.

He resolved to watch for any hint of daylight, in the direction from which the girl had entered. It was unlikely that there were two entrances, so that direction must lead to the ledge. He must know his surroundings as well as possible, in case he had a chance to escape. Which possibility, of course, seemed quite remote at the present time.

There was one moment when a resentful question rose in his mind. Where had his spirit-guide been when he had really needed it? The answer popped into his mind at once. There *had* been a warning, and he had been thinking of other things. *Aiee,* it was necessary to learn how to listen to one's spirit-guide. If, of course, he lived long enough for it to matter.

Despite his fears and his resolve to watch for the dawn, White Fox was exhausted from loss of sleep. The past two nights, as well as his injury, had taken a toll. He fell asleep, to dream confusing, frightening dreams which he could not even remember when he awoke.

That occurred after daylight. The girl was moving around the cave, and the fire was burning, small but brightly. She had just placed something on a stick to cook at the fire. It appeared to be one of the large frogs he had heard at the stream. She did not seem to be aware that he was awake, so he took advantage of that fact to look around.

The cave was about three paces wide and the same in depth. The roof varied, but in most areas was high enough for an average person to stand. Light reflected in from the opening, illuminating the entire cave. There seemed to be a sort of turn or twist to the entrance tunnel, so that he could not see the outside sky. At least, not from where he now lay. That would account for his impression of total blackness when he woke last night.

Against the other wall was a pile of robes that appeared to be the girl's bed. A bow and some arrows leaned against the wall. At the back of the cave were some racks of willow, which held a few rawhide storage packs, presumably supplies. He reflected that this girl must be a skillful hunter to support herself through a winter. Unless, of course, she could transform to a bear and hibernate.

At the far end, the cave narrowed to a crevice of indeterminate depth. It seemed to be a cleft in the rock that came from deep inside, and was lost again in the roof of the cave. He noticed that the trifling bit of smoke from the fire rose to that crevice, as to the smoke-hole of a skin lodge. It would probably circulate through this and other crevices, dissipating and perhaps mixing with the perpetual mists that some had observed around the Rock from a distance.

The girl turned and noticed that his eyes were open. For an instant she appeared startled, a little frightened, perhaps. Then her expression changed to one of determination. She said nothing, but made a brief hand-sign that indicated, "You are awake." She turned back to the fire.

"Who are you?" he asked.

She looked at him for a moment, gave a guttural grunt, and turned again to the fire.

He tried the same question again, this time in the tongue of the Head Splitters, then that of the Growers, even in the language of his mother's people from the pueblos. All attempts met with the same reaction. A startled look, an animal snarl or grunt. It was a little frightening, to have only animal sounds emerge from the throat of such a beautiful woman. He was still impressed that there was intelligence and wisdom in the dark eyes, as well as fear and doubt. But she seemed to make only animal sounds. What sort of wild creature was this, who could not speak? At least, who seemed to understand none of the various tongues he had tried.

She turned from the fire, holding the meat in one hand. With the other, she gave terse commands in hand-sign talk.

"Sit up! You eat, now."

With difficulty, he managed to prop himself against the wall, while the girl waited impatiently. As he did so, he was thinking rapidly. Sign talk! That was the answer. But his hands were tied.

# 13
>> >> >>

"**E**at!" The girl repeated the hand-sign.

White Fox gestured with his bound wrists and shrugged help-lessly. The girl paused in confusion for a moment, suspicion strong on her face. Then she seemed to realize that his implied request was reasonable. She drew her knife and stepped forward, with another snarl. With a slash she severed his fetters. The thongs fell away, to leave White Fox trying to rub circulation back into his hands.

"Eat!" she signed again, handing him the well-browned frog legs.

This was not an item in the usual diet of the People, but he was hungry. Besides, it was to his benefit to cooperate with this girl who was now his captor. He took the meat and almost dropped it; his hands were so numb from lack of circulation. Fox thought he saw a flicker of compassion in her eyes for a moment. He hoped that she would not feel it necessary to re-tie his hands. He wondered how he could appear as harmless as possible, and decided to move slowly, so as not to alarm the girl. He ate slowly, until she began to grunt impatiently, and then quickly finished and laid the bones aside.

"It is good," he signed. "How are you called?"

The girl's eyes widened perceptibly. She seemed astonished that he would know the hand-signs, but also still suspicious.

"No," she indicated, "how are *you* called?"

"I am White Fox, of the Elk-dog people."

"What are you doing here?"

"I came on my vision-quest. I did not know anyone's lodge was here."

"But you came back."

"Yes. I came to help you."

The girl snarled, baring her teeth.

"No!" she signed. "You lie! You hid and watched me!"

*Aiee*, he thought, she knew all along!

"But you tried to kill me, before!" he signed.

"Yes! You disturbed the bones of my grandfather!"

"I disturbed no one. I . . ."

He paused. This was not going well. He was making her angry.

"I did not know anyone was here," he signed more slowly and calmly. "I would not disturb anyone's burial. I was surprised, and stopped to see."

She appeared to ponder this.

"What is your tribe?" he asked.

"I have no tribe," she indicated.

"Is there no one?"

"Only my grandfather. He died in the Moon of Long Nights."

So, it was as he thought. The funeral-wrapped corpse had been there since midwinter.

"I am sorry," he gestured. "No one else?"

Again came the flash of fear and suspicion in her sensitive face.

"I need no one," she gestured defiantly.

He nodded. It was obvious that she was indeed quite self-suffi-
cient, at least in daily needs.

"You and your grandfather," Fox signed. "Have you been here
long?"

"We have been here always."

This was confusing.

"You have never seen others? Other people?"

Again, the look of defiance and distrust. Then she seemed to
soften a little.

"Sometimes they come here. We hide; they go away."

White Fox was beginning to see the implications of this conversation in hand-signs. This girl had lived here with the one she
called her grandfather since before she could remember, in fear
and distrust of all other people. It was a strange story. It must have
been that the grandfather was somewhat crazy, a recluse who had
left his people. But why did the girl seem to have no language,
other than the sign talk?

"Your grandfather," he asked, "talked with his mouth?"

Again came the look of suspicion.

"What do you mean?"

"People make sounds to talk."

He spoke the sentence as he signed it, and she was startled.
Then she regained her composure.

"You spoke with sounds, before," she signed. "I have heard
others do this."

Maybe she was unable to speak, he thought.

"But you?"

"Yes, but I do not need to."

She threw back her head and gave a little barking cry that
sounded like a coyote calling to her pups. Then she shrugged as if
to indicate that there was no purpose, and smiled, a little embarrassed.

"Your grandfather . . . did he make such sounds?"

He was trying to visualize a child, growing up with only a crazy
old man who made animal sounds.

"No, no," the girl signed. "He made no sound at all. He heard no sound."

Ah, so the grandfather was deaf! This explained her inability to speak. This girl had heard only the sounds of animal voices since she could remember. And occasionally, perhaps, distant scraps of spoken conversation by travelers who stopped here. Even that would have been infrequent, for there was a reluctance to remain near the Rock.

"But you hear sounds. You could make sounds, too."

"Why?"

"It is easier. Look, I am called 'White Fox.' "

He used the words as well as the signs.

"Now, how are you called?" he asked.

She seemed hesitant, as if by revealing her identity she would be losing something. Then she gave a shy smile.

"Grandfather called me South Wind," she gestured.

"It is good," Fox signed back. "South Wind."

He used the words as well as the hand-signs.

"White Fox," he said, pointing to his chest, "South Wind," pointing to her.

The girl smiled, showing even white teeth in a smile that seemed to light up the cave.

"South Wind," she said hesitantly, pointing to herself. She smiled again. "White Fox."

Fox nodded. He was pleased with the girl's reaction. She would learn rapidly. He reverted to hand-signs again.

"Did your grandfather tell you why he left his people?"

Her face darkened, the expression of fear and distrust returned. White Fox wished that he had not asked the question.

"Because people are bad! There is danger!" she signed heatedly.

"But, your grandfather was not bad. You are not bad. I am not bad!"

South Wind appeared to hesitate for a moment of confusion. Then she appeared to come to a decision.

"It is time to tie you again," she signed.

She picked up a rawhide cord and stepped toward him. Fox was not pleased at the unpleasant prospect of being tied again.

"Wait! If my hands are tied, we cannot talk!" he gestured frantically.

The girl paused.

"No," she signed. "You are a danger to me!"

"No, no! I want to help you!"

"You came back. You hid and wanted to catch me," she accused.

"Yes, but only to talk to you. You would run if I came to you. And, you tried to kill me before."

Again, she hesitated for a little while. He could see her indecision. If he could work on that, he felt that it was possible to reach her and learn more about her. There were still many questions here. Besides, he dreaded the helplessness that would result from being tied again. He considered trying to overpower her when she approached, but his ankles were still tied and he doubted if he could physically accomplish it. Besides, they were communicating fairly well, and he hated to lose that. He would surely destroy it if he tried to attack her.

"I thought you would disturb my grandfather," South Wind signed. "And, I was afraid you might be with the Evil One."

White Fox was startled. He felt a chill of fear up his spine. He had almost forgotten the terror of his first contact with the girl's spirit, during his vision-quest. It was quite disconcerting to learn from her that he was correct in his impressions. Even more so, the fact that he was learning in hand-sign talk, rather than words. The whole experience was eerie.

"South Wind," he gestured and used words together, remembering that it had seemed to please her. "I am not with the Evil One. I learned of your fears, and that is why I came back. I wanted to help you."

Even as he made the hand-signs, he could see that it was not successful. Her expression was changing, her lip curling in the defensive snarl.

"You lie!" she gestured angrily.

She seized his wrists and tied him expertly, despite his protests. Then she stood and faced him for a moment.

"Maybe you speak truth," she gestured, "but I do not know, so I must keep you tied. I go now."

She picked up her bow and left the cave.

White Fox struggled for a moment and then resigned himself to wait. He was quite frustrated. There was no way he could be of help if he was trussed up this way. There was no way he could even communicate with the girl. He had thought that things were moving well, but now he was back where he had started.

Well, not quite, perhaps. She had made one encouraging concession as she left.

"Maybe you speak truth."

# 14

>> >> >>

South Wind stepped along the familiar path on the ledge, more confused and troubled than at any time she could remember. She wished that she could talk to her grandfather.

It had been hard since his death, in the long nights of the Moon of Snows. Not so much the rigors of daily survival. She was used to that. For the past year, as she saw him growing weaker by the day, she had taken over the chores of survival. She had never known any other person, at least that she could remember. After his death, she had been completely alone, and the fears of childhood had returned to haunt her. She longed to be held again in the strong arms of her grandfather, who would rock gently to comfort her, as he had when she was small.

Her earliest memories were of living here on the Rock with her grandfather. Life was good. He fed her, comforted her after the bumps and scrapes of childhood, and taught her to hunt, to swim, and climb the rocky face of the cliff.

She swam in the clear waters of the river, played with the numerous bones that she found in the nooks and crannies of the rocky crevices. Grandfather had taken one buffalo thighbone and painted a face on its rounded end. Then he wrapped it in a scrap of fur, to resemble a bundled infant. The tiny girl had clapped her hands in delight over the doll, and had carried it everywhere with her. Her grandfather could always help with any situation that arose, comforting her fears and doubts.

But he was gone. She had done her best to care for his body, to prepare it for the crossing over of his spirit to the Other Side. He had told her of this, as he had told her of many other things of their people through the years. There were stories, told with hand-signs by the light of the fire during long winter days and nights when the trail on the cliff was impassable with ice and snow. She had learned that there were other tribes, besides the one from which they came. She knew in detail the customs of her own, and some of the others' ways. She had been fascinated to learn of other people, as she grew to young womanhood.

It was at about that time that she realized that something was wrong about her grandfather's approach to all this. He would tell her in detail, with almost loving memory in his face, about their people. She would ask something like, "Where are they now?" and he would fly into a rage, telling her in frantic sign talk that people are not to be trusted. All of them, yes, all tribes, are full of lies and deceit, and she must always avoid contact with them.

That approach had seemed reasonable as a small child. She had played the game of hiding on the few occasions when people came to the Rock, perhaps even to camp overnight. Sometimes she was confused by the fact that they seemed happy among themselves. They made strange, complicated sounds to speak to each other, somewhat like those of the birds or the coyotes. She asked Grandfather about this and he explained about his own affliction, that he could hear nothing. He made some sounds, but they seemed to have no meaning, beyond the simple tones of approval, irritation, or love.

"We do not need such sounds," he explained to her.

"But they seem happy," she had observed.

Grandfather had become irritated, as he sometimes did when she asked about their people.

"That is part of their deceit," he signed irritably. "We do not need them." He smiled at her. "We have each other."

When she was small, that had been sufficient, but as she matured, she became more curious. She found that she could inquire about the customs of other people, up to a point. When she saw him start to become irritable, she would immediately change the subject. In this way, little by little, she had learned much. She already knew that not everyone lived in caves in a cliff. Now she pressed for knowledge of other dwellings, of customs and traditions, of stories of creation.

She began to understand from some of the stories that it must be that not *every* other person was evil, only most of them. All of them, of course, when Grandfather was in one of his tirades. Then there was nothing but to watch the hand-signs and nod agreeably.

It was almost as bad when she began to be curious about her parents. She could observe the animals and their young, and began to question her own parentage. The reaction on the part of her grandfather, when she would approach this subject, was even more unpleasant than his anger. He would cry great tears, rock from side to side in his anguish, and repeatedly make the signs for "dead, all dead!" She would hug and comfort him, and eventually he would feel better.

"But I have you!" he would sign as he dried his tears.

She could not remember when the Evil One was first mentioned. It was about the time that his health began to fail. During that time, several moons before his death, he seemed to be two different people. At times, he would sadly tell her all she wished to ask. At other times, he would become completely irrational, signing confusing and meaningless gestures, some of which appeared to be names of people he had never mentioned before. At such times, his eyes would seem to lose their contact with reality, and he would stare and point at things not there. It was frightening, and she was glad that it had not happened when she was small. This was also about the time that he began to mention the Evil One. Gradually, it seemed that all of the evil, lying, and deceit in the world began to draw itself together in his mind, to become one person, the Evil One.

"You must beware of him," the old man would sign, his eyes glittering in the firelight.

South Wind realized that something was wrong with his mind, and it was a terrible time.

However, during his more lucid intervals, he seemed to recognize a sense of urgency. He finally confided to her that he was dying, which she already suspected. He instructed her in burial preparation for when the time would come.

She also found that when he was in one of these moods, he could be quite communicative. She could push for information which would once have made him recoil in anger or in grief. Now, it was possible to question gently and to obtain answers. For the first time he was able to reveal how the two of them came to the Rock.

A small group of the People, he said in hand-signs, were camped somewhat farther east than usual one summer. They were attacked by a fierce band of Forest People, and all were killed. He had snatched up his infant granddaughter and hidden in the bushes while the killing and mutilation went on.

"Your parents, your grandmother, all of them," he signed sadly.

"But, Grandfather, why did you not go back to others of our people?"

"No," he signed, with the old anger coming to the front again. "They left us. They are full of lies and deceit."

She knew that it was time to change the subject. But now, there was some satisfaction in knowing of her parents. Her mother—she did not even know her name—had been the daughter of the Grandfather who now referred to himself as "He-Who-Mourns."

She had chosen as a burial place the wide spot on the ledge

where she had played as a child, and where they had loved to sit together to watch the sunsets. Now she paused, as she did each time she passed. She sat for a moment on the boulder near the wrapped corpse.

"Grandfather," she signed, "much has happened. I wish you were here to tell me what I must do."

She paused, to look up and down the river. Once, life had been so simple. Now, so complicated and confusing. Even before the coming of the young man who called himself White Fox, she had begun to have doubts about the outside world, and whether there was a place in it for her. She had been able to decide that the whole world could not be evil. Otherwise, how could her grandfather have been kind and good? And surely, her mother? Grandfather had demonstrated love and affection when he told that story, so there were *some* good people.

But how did one tell? If her grandfather were here . . . but no, he had never been willing to admit this possibility, that of people who were good.

Then there was the newcomer, who was exciting, yet seemed kind, and who seemed to want to help her. She had been alarmed when he camped at the top of the cliff, and prepared to stay a little while. She had crept close, closer than she had ever been to anyone before, and watched him sleep. White Fox, he had called himself. He was good to look at, and she had felt a strange exhilaration when she lifted him to carry his limp form to the cave. His muscles were firm and well developed, and his face handsome. She hoped that she had not hurt him badly.

It was pleasant to talk to him, and she would do so again, but just now she must get out, away from him, to think a little.

There were other problems in her life just now. She did not understand her recurrent dreams. They had become more frequent and more terrifying since her grandfather's death. Dreams of the formless, dark being that Grandfather had called the Evil One. South Wind felt somehow that, all her life, the only protection between her and the dark Thing had been her grandfather. Now, that protection was gone, and she could feel the evil growing stronger. Now she hated to sleep at night. She felt safer when it was light, and spent more time now catnapping during the day. Conversely, she prowled more at night. This helped to avoid the dreams of the Evil One.

She wondered how White Fox knew of the Evil One. At least, he had suggested that he did. He seemed to understand some things about her. She was glad that she had not killed him, as she had considered doing. He seemed kind and understanding, and she found herself wishing that Grandfather could have known White Fox. Then he could have advised her how to proceed.

There were many things that she liked about the young man. It was exciting to be spoken to with sounds. She smiled to herself as she remembered that he had spoken her name, the only person who had ever done so. The sound of it was good when he said it. She spoke it now, softly and to herself.

"South Wind."

She smiled again.

# 15

>> >> >>

"**I** will be back, Grandfather," she signed, and moved on along the ledge.

It was part of her daily ritual, the pause to speak to her grandfather. It was a reassurance to her, as much as an honor to the dead. There was comfort and security, of a sort, in having cared for her grandfather in his declining days, and then having been able to care properly for him at death. She realized that this was not a usual thing for the rest of the world. However, she was intelligent enough to realize that her life was not a usual thing. Increasingly she wondered what it would be like to live among other people. It was frightening to think of, yet there were many people who did live so. Everyone, she had come to believe, except her and Grandfather.

She stepped onto the grassy strip at the bottom of the cliff, and glanced at the dogwood thicket where she had attacked and captured the young man . . . White Fox. That had been easy. She had known that he was hiding to watch her, and reasoned that he must mean harm to her. She must act first. There was no good reason to explain why she had captured, instead of killing him. It was just a whim, and maybe a little loneliness for companionship. She had actually enjoyed having him at the top of the Rock for a few days. She could hide and watch him. He would have left without even knowing of her existence if he had not accidently discovered Grandfather. She had panicked and attacked him. That was a close escape for both of them, the fall from the cliff.

She had thought him dead. Her search up and down the stream revealed no trace, and this was a puzzling thing. She was still wondering over that when the man appeared again. It seemed that he had been away from the Rock for maybe two sleeps, and then returned. South Wind had almost overlooked him, hiding there among the sumac stems. Well, she would let him stay there for a while, she had decided. It was rather amusing to think of his discomfort, there in the heat of the day, with the mosquitoes attacking his bare skin at every opportunity.

Now that she had captured him, she did not quite know what to do. He did not seem so frightening as he had earlier. It had not really occurred to her until the episode in the cave that she could talk to him. Not only in signs, but in sounds! That had been exciting, and unexpected. She wanted more.

Just now, she had another task. She must hunt, to feed the two of them. The frog had been only an overture, a temporary thing, to show her willingness to forget the violence of their previous encounters.

It was much like the time she had captured a coyote pup. Her grandfather had consented for her to keep it, but cautioned her about the responsibility to it. She must feed it. The animal was interesting to play with, and provided a degree of happiness that was different from the ordinary, during many days that summer.

Then the pup matured. During the Moon of Madness, when all of the earth's creatures behave strangely, the coyote did, also. When the long lines of geese began to honk their way south, the pup seemed restless. It began to forage farther from the Rock, and no longer played with the girl. Finally, one day, it failed to return.

There was perhaps, South Wind thought, an extended similarity here. She must feed and water her captive, and even though it was pleasurable to play with the sounds that had the same meanings as hand-signs, she still felt a danger. Just as she had sometimes been bitten by the pup, there could be danger with this young man. When she had gone to Grandfather with tears in her eyes to show him her injuries, he would comfort her and remind her that such is the way of life. For each pleasure there are responsibilities, efforts, small hurts and dangers.

She was not quite sure what the danger to her might be from this young man. Surely he would not bite, like the coyote. This thought affected her with a strange excitement which puzzled her. She had watched coyotes and foxes among their own, playing and wrestling, nipping each other, sometimes roughly. It had seemed to her that this was a show of affection. Her grandfather had often tossed her playfully in his arms when she was small, and when she grew too big for such games, it was a disappointment.

She might not have thought of this at all, except for another sensation that was a new feeling for her. During the first encounter on the ledge, as she wrestled with the intruder, he had grasped her knife-wrist with great strength. No one had ever grasped her before. Her encounters of skill and strength had been with animals which she sought for food. They might kick with sharp hooves, strike with horns or antlers, or even bite. But she had never been grasped before. She had been unable to break the grip until after they fell and struck the water.

There was the other sensation, too, which was still puzzling to her. As they rolled in combat on the shelf, and she tried to pinion her adversary with her legs, there was a strange excitement. He had managed to roll from under her, because he was heavier, and very strong. As she felt his weight upon her body, pressing on her breasts and stomach, there was a moment of exhilaration that was almost pleasurable. She had puzzled much over that sensation in the ensuing days. She tried to deny it, but decided that it really had been there. It was only for an instant, before they had gone over the edge and the struggle became one of survival again.

Her thoughts were distracted for a moment by a movement in the clearing ahead. She froze, watching. Ah, yes! The three rabbits were engaged in a courtship dance, and would be careless. She fitted an arrow to her bowstring and waited a little while. She would be able to kill one, if she used care. Some time soon, she must try to kill a deer, or even a buffalo if she could. She must dry enough meat for the coming winter months.

This brought her back to the thought of the young man lying trussed in the cave. She was hunting now for two. It was pleasant to do so. She had hunted for both her own needs and those of her grandfather for a long time as his health had failed. Now, it was good to do so again. To share the results of her efforts. This man might be dangerous, but surely not an ally of the Evil One. He seemed to know about that, and in fact had offered to help. That was a very comforting thing, somehow. She did not completely understand why the Evil One seemed to be growing stronger.

It was largely since her grandfather's death, and she had been unaware of it at first. Since she was small, she had had a fear of the dark crevice at the back of the little cave. There were the frightening dreams, of some Thing lurking there which would come out to do harm. She would cry out and waken, and Grandfather would hold and rock and comfort her, and the fears would go away.

As she grew older, it became possible to ignore such thoughts. That is, until her grandfather's mind began to fail. Then, it seemed to let down a defense of some sort. *He* became the one with fears, with terror, even. Again, she thought, in the last few moons before his death, he had seemed to take all evil everywhere, all the evil created by and experienced by the human race, and lump it together in his failing, childlike mind. It became the Evil One.

Most of the time, she had been able to understand that this was the product of his failing, childlike thoughts. He was becoming a child again. She was sure of this when he would call her "Mother," or by a name of someone he may have mentioned long ago. It was frightening, but she knew that things happen so. It was almost a relief when it was over for him, the pain as well as the confusion.

It was only a few nights after his death that the recurrent dream of her childhood returned. The dark Thing seemed to ooze out of the crevice and she had awakened in terror, uncertain not only where she was, but *who* she was. Outside the cave on the ledge, drawing cold air into her lungs, the fear seemed ridiculous. She had returned to her bed and slept again, mildly amused at her fearful dream. It was a childish thing, caused, no doubt, by her recent loss.

She was able to accept that for a while, but the dreams returned, a little more threatening. It became a larger problem. If, as she had assumed, the fears of the evil in the dark crevice were those of childhood, what was happening now? The fears had been there when she was small, and had returned for her grandfather as he became a child again. Now, they should be gone, as no child was now here. Instead, the evil was growing stronger. It was becoming not the vague Thing that hid in the crevice to creep out when she slept. It was as Grandfather kept signing in his last days, a *person*, the Evil One. She felt sometimes that her only protection, all her life, had been her grandfather's sheer force of will. Without him, she had no defense against whatever horror might lurk in the crevice. And whatever it might be, the formless Thing of her childhood or the Evil One of her grandfather's last days, it *was* growing stronger.

One of the rabbits paused and froze in a good position for a shot. South Wind drew the arrow to its tip and released it. The string twanged, and two of the rabbits scuttled to cover. The third lay kicking in the grass. She hurried forward to retrieve it and turned back toward the cave.

It was good to think of having someone to return to. She would untie his hands, maybe even his feet, and talk to him. She would learn the sounds that meant the same as hand-signs. It would be good, the companionship. She had not realized how she had missed that, simply the presence of another spirit.

Yes, there might be some problems, as there had been with the coyote pup, but she could handle them. By the time she reached the cave, she had decided. It would be worth the slight risks that she recognized, the problems involved with having this man, White Fox, in her lodge.

Yes, she would keep him awhile.

# 16

>> >> >>

**W**hite Fox lay in the cave, the fetters chafing his wrists and ankles. He was frustrated and angry. Why, he asked himself, had he ever considered coming back to this place? He should have been grateful for his escape, and ready to forget the whole bizarre experience and go on with his life.

Yet, even in his discomfort and frustration, he knew he could not have done so. The girl, South Wind, drew him like a moth to flame. He had managed to establish communication, and now knew a little more about her. It was an incredible story, one with which he could sympathize. He could hardly imagine a lifetime with only one other person, or the tragedy over his loss.

His own position was still precarious, he knew. This strange girl could easily decide to kill him, just to remove any imagined danger to herself. She had tried to kill him once, and he had no doubt that she was capable of it. She had nearly succeeded. In fact, he was alive now only by good luck. And, of course, the help of his spirit-guide.

He rolled over, to ease his cramped muscles, without much success. At least, he thought, there was some progress. He had managed to obtain enough information to begin to understand something of the girl. To begin with, she was not actually crazy, as he had once feared. Her grandfather may have been. Probably was crazy, he decided. Otherwise, why would he have carried off an infant girl, and rejected all human contact for the rest of his life? Judging from her appearance, the girl had just reached womanhood. Even so, the two had lived in the Rock for at least fifteen or sixteen seasons. It was remarkable, actually, that South Wind was *not* crazy. At least, no more so than she appeared to be.

He was still astonished at her appearance. There had been a little while, as they conversed in hand-sign talk, when he had been able to appreciate her remarkable beauty close at hand. She had exhibited practically no shyness about her body, and he felt intrigued by her freedom of movement. He longed to learn more about her, to teach her the words that she had never heard. She had seemed to delight in hearing and speaking her own name.

He sighed in frustration at the thought that he had no control over the situation at the moment. Even his ability to communicate depended on the whim of the girl. He could not use sign talk with his hands tied. Besides, there were other problems, one of which was rapidly increasing in urgency. He had not had an opportunity to empty his bladder since his capture, and he was becoming quite uncomfortable. This was evident when he moved, yet the pressure made it difficult to remain still. He tried not to think about it. The best way to remove something from his mind was to think of something else, he knew, but it was impossible to think of anything else. He was beginning to wonder how long he could withstand the increasing pressure when he heard the sound of the girl's returning footsteps on the ledge.

She entered, smiled at him, and held up a freshly killed rabbit. White Fox smiled back and nodded eagerly, holding up his hands to ask his release. The girl seemed to consider for a moment, then nodded agreement. As quickly as he could, Fox signed to indicate his predicament, and pointed to his feet, still bound.

"I will not try to run away," he signed.

The girl looked doubtful again for a moment, and then nodded. White Fox was already loosening the ties on his ankles. He stood, and almost fell as a thousand needles stabbed at his feet with the returning circulation. With difficulty, he hobbled to the ledge outside the cave to relieve himself. He was dimly aware that the girl stood in the entrance to make certain he did not flee.

Finally, he turned back toward the cave to find her standing there.

"I am sorry," she signnd. "I did not think."

"It is nothing," he indicated, though it was not true.

His feet and legs were moving better now, and he stepped inside past her. His eyes became accustomed to the dim light, and he looked around from this new vantage point. Over by the supply racks lay his medicine pouch and his weapons. At that point the girl touched him on the shoulder, and he turned.

"No," she signed. "If you try, I will tie you again."

White Fox was willing to take her at her word. He might be able to overpower her, but it would accomplish nothing, and would ruin the trust that was beginning to grow between them.

"I will cook meat," she signed as she dropped to her knees to finish butchering out the rabbit.

In a short while, it was cooking on a spit over the fire, and she turned again to him.

"Now," she gestured, "tell me more of the talk-sounds."

Patiently, White Fox introduced words, illustrating them with hand-signs. She learned rapidly, chuckling with delight at some of the sounds that stood for familiar things.

"Did your grandfather ever mention your tribe . . . its name?" he asked in signs, after she began to tire.

"No, I do not think so. Grandfather always said we had no tribe."

"But you were with other people. Some were killed, and the others ran away. You told it."

"Yes, that is true. I do not know."

"Let me show you signs for names of tribes," he suggested. "See if any look right."

Painstakingly, he tried the sign for every tribe he knew. Growers, Forest People, Pawnee, Mandan, Head Splitters, even the pueblo tribes of his mother's people. She shook her head.

"Maybe the Forest People are the ones who killed us," she considered.

One last possibility occurred to him.

"This?" he asked, making the sign for a man on a horse.

The girl's eyes widened.

"Yes!" she signed eagerly. "Yes, that is the one!"

White Fox was astonished.

"Really? Elk-dog People?"

"Yes," she nodded. "Grandfather used the sign, a man on a horse."

"That is my own tribe!" Fox signed. "We call ourselves 'the People,' but others use the elk-dog sign, because the People used the horse long ago."

He could hardly believe it. The girl was of his own people. He tried to think. Surely, there must have been a story about the incident . . . a dim light stirred in his memory . . . yes, when he was quite small. A family or two of the Eastern Band had quarreled with the others, and had camped apart from them. They had not returned, and a search party that fall had found only bones. He had heard this story. His grandmother had been of the Eastern Band. People made jokes about the foolish ways of that band, but his father, Red Feather, took pride in his heritage. That was why the story of this incident was discussed very little, he supposed.

"Then I am of your people?" South Wind was asking in hand-talk.

"Yes," he nodded. "I think so. My grandmother, who died long ago, was of your band, and her father was a chief."

The girl clapped her hands, delighted.

"It is good!"

White Fox smiled. He found this trace of childlike simplicity in a strong, capable woman an intriguing trait. He sat, massaging his sore wrists and ankles. He was trying not to be too obvious with his glances at the beauty of her face and the graceful curves of her long legs and body.

She saw the reddened stripes on his wrists and her face fell.

"I am sorry," she signed.

White Fox dismissed her concern with a casual gesture.

"It is nothing."

When the rabbit had finished cooking, South Wind divided it in half, and handed him a portion. Then she came and sat beside him. There was a new and strange closeness, a communication without words. It seemed that the discovery of who she was, where she had come from, was important to the girl. She was now more relaxed and cheerful. There seemed to be a trust not previously found here.

They finished eating, and she made no effort to retie him. Suddenly she jumped to her feet.

"Let us swim!" she signed, starting for the entrance.

White Fox rose to follow her. Even though she paused a moment to speak in signs to her grandfather, she reached the shore well ahead of him. Quickly, she stripped the shirt-like dress over her head and dived headfirst into the pool. Fox followed, quite self-consciously at first. They swam, splashed, and cavorted like otters in the clear water, laughing like delighted children, and it was good. White Fox's cares were cleansed away, like the sweat and accumulated grime from his skin. He completely forgot, for a little while, the ominous reason for his presence here, and he was a child again, enjoying the swim, the day, and a pleasant companion.

Even as they played, she was asking and learning. A small green heron croaked its raucous cry, and she lifted a right hand in the question sign.

"Heron," he answered aloud. "Little green heron."

"Green?" she asked.

"Yes. A color. Like trees, grass."

"Green!"

She laughed, a delightful musical laugh, like a rippling bird song.

They grew tired, and waded from the stream to lie on the sandy strip of beach in the sun. This was most difficult for White Fox. He longed to touch her, to take her in his arms and hold her close, but he dared not. The risk of rejection was more than merely rejection. If any action on his part happened to offend her, she could easily fly into a rage such as he had already experienced. After all, though their communication had been progressing well, he could not forget that he was still her prisoner.

The shadows were lengthening when she rose and picked up her tunic. Fox watched as she gracefully tossed it up and slipped it over her head, settling the garment over her shoulders and hips. She walked upstream a few steps to the riffle and knelt to drink, then started toward the path.

"Come," she gestured.

Fox rose and dressed quickly, to follow her back to the cave. He was confused, and had no idea what to expect next. The girl was a complete contradiction in all that she did. A wonderful, delightfully childish yet capable contradiction. Here he was, following her bidding like a slave, but because he wanted to.

Strange, he thought to himself. They had not even begun to approach the reason for his being here.

# 17

>> >> >>

**W**hen South Wind fell asleep that night, she was happier and more confident than at any time since her grandfather's passing. The sheer emotional strength of another person's presence was reassuring. It was like the protective feeling that she had felt when she was small and would take her tears to Grandfather for comfort. Now, it was not the tears of bumps and scrapes and minor disappointments. She had outgrown all that. No, she thought, this was more like the reassurance that Grandfather's presence had provided when her night terrors had wakened her as a child. Or, maybe, her irrational fear of the dark crevice at the back of the cave.

In the clear light of day, she had always been able to reason that there was nothing there, and she was not afraid, even when she was small. It was only after dark, by the flickering light of the fire, that she would begin to wonder. She would cast quick glances at some half-seen movement in the shadows, and there would be nothing. But the uneasy suspicion would remain. Or she would dream, and waken in terror, to run to Grandfather's bed for safety and comfort. He would hold her and rock gently, and lay a few sticks on the fire. The blaze would bring light to the cave, and everything would be safe and happy again.

In time, she had outgrown the fears, and they had not returned until Grandfather's mind started to fail. Then it was as if the dark Thing in the rock had been there all along, held at bay by the two spirits of South Wind and the old man. As Grandfather's spirit weakened, the dark Thing seemed to grow stronger. Yes, that must be it. It required the force of two spirits to hold the Evil One at bay. The loss of Grandfather had so weakened her defense that it had become a danger. She had been able to avoid it by leaving the cave when the dark presence became too overpowering.

Tonight, though, there would be no need. She had a companion. She had enjoyed, even reveled in, the excitement of learning the word-sounds, and he had enjoyed it, too. She had seen that in the expression of his face, the light in his eyes. He was happy when he was with her.

She began to fantasize. They would stay here, sharing the cave together. They would be happy, and they would never need anyone else. White Fox would be her husband. She was not completely certain what that involved, but her grandfather's stories had implied that usually, a man and a woman live together. Her heart told her that would be good. Maybe White Fox would know more about it. She already had a feeling that it would feel good to be held in the arms of White Fox, as her grandfather used to hold her. No, it would be different. The feeling she perceived when she thought of White Fox was warm and tender and protective, and . . . well, it was *different.* Maybe she could ask him about it.

The fire was dying, and she lay there in the darkness, listening to the deep, regular breathing of the young man. She was too excited to sleep. She longed to waken him to talk some more, but felt it would be inappropriate. At least, she told herself with satisfaction, she would not need to leave the cave tonight, to escape the influence of the Thing in the crevice. The combined strength of the two of them could deny it entry, could bar it from the cave.

There had been no thought of tying him tonight. After the day they had spent together, she could not find it in herself to distrust him. Besides, he had shown no sign that he would be dangerous. None, even, that he wished to leave. That helped with her fantasy about living here forever together. Maybe she should mention that tomorrow.

She regretted, now that she knew him better, that she had left him tied in the cave that first night. That had been a bad thing to do, to leave him helpless with the Thing while she went prowling. It could have been dangerous to him, and she was glad that he was safe. She would not do anything like that again. She only hoped that he would forgive her, and he seemed to have done so. At least, if he held resentment, he probably would not have been so pleasant to talk to.

She finally fell asleep, with a warm comfortable feeling that all was well. There was a companion only an arm's length away, who could be of help in an emergency. It was the most secure that she had felt for many moons. It felt almost as good as sleeptime had when she was a child.

It was perhaps not surprising, then, that after a period of deep sleep, she began to dream, and saw herself as a child. She and Grandfather walked along the stream, and he taught her to hunt and to shoot, and to swim like the beavers. Days were long and happy. She played again on the rocky ledges with her coyote pup, and felt the twinge of sadness when it ran away. She relived the long nights in the Moon of Snows when they stayed in the cave. They wrapped themselves warmly against the onslaught of Cold Maker, and huddled over the tiny fire that must not be allowed to go out. That was a time for Grandfather's stories, and she learned of other people.

She dreamed of the games they played when others came to the Rock, and how she must remain hidden and quiet until they left. All of these were happy dreams.

Then came the one with the old fear. She was still a child in this dream, but alone in the cave. Her grandfather would be back soon, but night was falling. Carefully, she placed a little stick on the coals of the fire, and it blazed up to throw a flickering light around the rough walls. The little girl looked apprehensively toward the dark crevice and shuddered. There had never been anything there when she looked, and there was not now. She looked away, resolved not to look again. But the flicker of the fire made little shadowy movements, which she saw out of the corner of her eye. She would look quickly, and the movement was gone. There was nothing there but the dark crevice.

She looked anxiously to the doorway, hoping to see the tall form of her grandfather against the dull smoke-gray of the twilight sky. There was no indication of his return. What if he *never* returned?

She whimpered softly in her sleep, like a child, and the dream continued. There came a time when her glance at the dark corner *almost* revealed something. A flickering, slithering Thing that moved briefly and was gone, a part of the rough rock of the crevice and the flicker of firelight.

Fascinated, she stared at the crack, like the bird who is stalked by the snake. Horrified, she watched a formless shadow vaporize, spewing from the crevice, like smoke or mist, but dark, dirty brown-black. There was an odor, too, of slime and decay, and a sense of evil that grew, threatening to fill the cave.

The little girl screamed out in terror and scrambled toward the entrance to escape. She ran headlong into the arms of Grandfather as he entered. He rocked and held her tenderly, and she felt secure again. Her sobs began to subside, and Grandfather reached to place a stick on the fire. Flames produced more light, and the cave brightened.

Then she was awake and no longer a child. The man who had placed the stick on the coals, into whose arms she had fled, was not Grandfather, but White Fox. He held her in his arms and rocked back and forth, crooning soft words of comfort. It did not seem to matter. She clung to him, as her terror slowly subsided, holding her arms tightly around him, fearing to let go. She felt that if she did, he might disappear, and she would be defenseless again.

She could look over his shoulder and see the back of the cave in the flickering light of the fire. The crevice was once more only a crack in the rock, and there was no horribly evil brown mist from her dream of the past to threaten the little girl. It had been only a dream, as had her night terrors of childhood. And, as her grandfather had dispelled her fears then, the man in her arms had done so now.

She released him from her embrace, and he did so, too, a little reluctantly it seemed.

"I am sorry," she signed. "A dream . . ."

He nodded, sleepily.

"It is over now," he assured her.

Yes, she thought, it is over. Only a false vision in the night. A little embarrassed, she turned to pick up the robe she had flung aside, and spread it to return to sleep.

Only one thing puzzled her a little bit. Why did there still seem to be a slight odor in the cave? An odor of putrefaction and slime and decay? That, she had thought, was part of the dream.

# 18

》》》

"**Y**ou must go! Now!"

Her statement could not have been stronger if it had been in words, but it was in sign talk. Although she had been enjoying the novelty of words and sounds, when she became serious, she reverted to her first language, hand-signs.

"No! Both of us!" insisted White Fox.

She shook her head angrily.

"No. It is my problem, not yours. You must go!"

"But you do not have to stay. Come with me."

She began to cry.

"I cannot go. My grandfather is here."

"But he is dead. You have done for him, mourned him; it is time to leave him. It is the way of the People."

The girl paused a moment to consider that.

"It is?" she asked.

"Of course. Now, come with me!"

"No, I cannot," she insisted. "I know no other place."

White Fox was becoming increasingly frustrated.

"I will help you," he pleaded. "You must leave. There is danger here for you."

"No. I stay. The danger would follow me."

He had not thought of that. White Fox had been quite impressed with the incident in the night. To be wakened by the sudden rush of the girl into his arms was, to say the least, disconcerting. He had spent the previous day with her, enjoying her company completely. He had longed to touch her, but dared not. On retiring, he lay for a little while, thinking of all the changes in the past day. The main purpose of his being here was all but forgotten in the joy of her company, her quickness in learning, her rippling laugh, and her overwhelming beauty. He would have gladly spent another day, any number of days, even a lifetime, he felt, with this girl. But he must move cautiously. If she became distrustful, his progress so far was wasted.

White Fox had become preoccupied with the immediate goal, that of communicating with her. He had thought of nothing beyond that, of what the next step might be.

They prepared to go to bed, and she did not mention tying him again. That was very good. He would not have absolutely refused, but he was glad he did not have to make a point of it. He expected to lie awake, thinking of the girl so near and yet so far, wishing to touch her, but knowing that it could destroy all his progress. Despite all this turmoil, he did fall asleep at once. The stresses on his body were too much, and he had not slept well for many nights.

He was awakened by the rush of the girl into his arms. At first he thought she was attacking him again, and seized her to defend himself. As he came up out of his sleep, he realized that she was crying out in fear, clinging to him for help. Almost instinctively, his arms encircled her, comforting and protecting, and she responded, clinging to him like a frightened child. Not until he tossed the sticks onto the fire for light did she begin to calm. She had been dreaming, and had rushed into his arms for defense against her fears. They had both been embarrassed, and had said very little before returning to bed and a restless remainder to the night.

This morning they had talked. White Fox, his attention once more on the purpose of his mission, tried to persuade her to leave the Rock with him. He was now meeting her unshakable resolve. He was also feeling more of the fear that he had perceived in his dream state during his vision-quest. There was an inkling of the stark terror that had awakened him from sleep during his fast. He had attributed that to his accidental encounter with the spirit of the girl, when he experienced her fear of the Evil Thing. Now he began to wonder about it.

He had felt a moment of terror when she seized and clung to him in his sleep. He had thought he was being attacked. But there was another fear for a moment, before the fire blazed into light and drove the shadows back into the corners of the cave. He felt that he had, for only a little while, experienced the influence of the Thing himself, rather than through the terror of the girl. It was a fearsome experience, one which had caused him to push for an immediate departure.

White Fox expected resistance, but was not prepared for the complete refusal he was meeting. Only gradually was he realizing the depth of the girl's fear of the outside world. Though it seemed incredible, she must fear other humans even more than she feared the Evil One. He wondered now that he had ever managed to talk to her at all.

Now South Wind had introduced a new objection to leaving. If she did leave, she now suggested that this Evil Thing she feared would *follow* her. White Fox felt a chill creep up the back of his neck as he considered that possibility. It was so great a threat that he almost overlooked the fact that she had *considered* leaving for a moment. But that moment was gone, and he was trying to deal with her suggestion that the Evil would follow her. Here in the bright light of a beautiful summer day, the terror of the night seemed far away. Yet, his brief sensation of contact with the fearsome Thing, between sleep and waking, made him take the idea quite seriously.

"It would follow you?" he asked.

"Yes, I think so . . . it grows stronger."

Again he felt the chilling sensation. His neck hairs started to prickle. If the Evil Thing would follow her, might it follow him, also? He had thought that the fear was in her mind, but maybe it was in the Rock itself. If that was true, and it was growing stronger . . . what if it had been in the Rock, and was about to escape into the outside world? He must know more about this.

"South Wind, where is it, this Evil Thing?"

"In the crack at the back of the cave, maybe."

"You have *seen* it?"

"No. Well, maybe . . . last night, in my dream."

"That is the first time?"

"Yes, but it is stronger now."

"When did it become stronger?"

"When Grandfather became a child again. Much more, since he crossed over."

White Fox paused to think a moment.

"When did you first know of the Evil?" he asked.

"When I was very small. I was afraid of the dark corner in the crevice. Grandfather told me it was nothing, and when I grew older, it was not there."

Ah, he thought, it *was* in her mind.

"Then it came back, later?" he asked.

"Yes. Grandfather felt it, too."

"Did he *see* it?"

"No. I did not, either, until last night. That was in a dream."

"Wind, how do you know it is growing stronger?"

She shrugged, with a sad smile.

"I can tell. It could not come out, all the time I was growing up. Then when it came back, we could keep it in, together. When Grandfather was sick, it was stronger. When he was gone, I had to fight it alone, and it grew."

"And now?"

"I thought that your spirit helped some. Two spirits, like mine and Grandfather's. But maybe not. It is strong. It would follow me. I know."

"But *how* do you know?"

"Because it is stronger. Last night I *smelled* it."

That, he realized, could not happen in a dream. Could it be that the girl was completely crazy? He thought not. Nothing else suggested such a thing. Her grandfather might have been crazy, probably was. But, except for this obsession of the Evil Thing in the crevice, South Wind seemed rational. As rational, at least, as one could be when raised in such strange circumstances.

And, he was inclined to believe her story. Surely it was possible for a childhood fear, long since outgrown, to return in the mind of the aging grandfather, whose mind was weakening. The grandfather's mind had been warped, apparently by tragedy, long ago, and carried the memories of fear and distrust. Finally, it all became centered on this nameless Thing, feeding and strengthening it, feeding its life in the mind of the girl. As her insecurity over her loss increased, so did the fearful Thing. He began to understand that she could not leave it behind, because it was in her mind. Yes, it would follow her. She would have to overcome it before she could leave, or it would remain with her.

His heart went out to her as he thought of the dark winter nights when she crouched in the cave in terror. She had been newly alone, afraid to sleep. Afraid to look at the crevice, yet afraid *not* to. It was not surprising that the Thing would grow in such a situation.

South Wind was hand-signing again now, bringing him back from his wandering thoughts. Her manner was somewhat calmer now.

"You go on," she was signing. "I must fight this myself, here at the Rock."

White Fox shook his head.

"I know you must stay," he agreed, "but I will stay to help you."

"No, no," she insisted, "there is danger to you."

"And to you!" he insisted. "But, you have said that you could control the Evil Thing when there were two of you. Now, *we* are two. We become stronger. Together we will kill it."

"Maybe . . ." she hesitated. "Maybe we could . . ."

White Fox nodded eagerly.

"We can!"

He wished that he could be as certain as that. Of one thing he was sure. South Wind could never do it alone. No one could.

# 19

>> >> >>

They considered moving out of the cave with the dark crevice.

"Are there other caves?" White Fox asked.

"Yes. None as good as this," she signed.

This struck him as amusing. Their entire problem revolved around the dark Thing in the back of this cave, yet South Wind seriously thought that there was no better place. He chuckled, and the girl, seeing the contradiction, laughed too, the delightful, liquid sound that he had noted before.

"No," she protested, "the other caves are smaller, no shelter at all, or too narrow, or they leak rain."

She paused, serious now.

"This has always been my lodge."

He nodded, understanding. He had always lived in a lodge of skins and poles, but his mother's people lived in adobe mud-brick houses. He could understand this girl's alarm at such a serious move.

They rejected that idea, but decided on a general change in daily routine. They would do most of their sleeping during daylight hours, and spend little time in the cave after dark.

"You should not be alone in the cave," White Fox suggested.

"You, either!" the girl insisted.

White Fox started to protest, but agreed that it was a good idea. In bright daylight, it might be safe, but after dark they should stay together, and neither should go into the cave alone.

With these precautions, understood by both, they could relax. Now they settled into a daily routine, which became quite pleasant to White Fox. The girl "introduced" him formally to her grandfather's still form on the ledge, explaining in signs what they were attempting. White Fox, ill at ease, signed also, using the term of respect among the People for any adult male.

"Greetings, Uncle. It is my privilege to help South Wind."

There was, of course, no response from the burial-wrapped form, and for this Fox was grateful. Despite the fact that he was becoming desperately fond of the young woman, he was still troubled by such things as her daily sign talk with Grandfather. However, he soon noticed that it seemed less important to her each day. Soon, she merely waved a greeting as she passed. That was understandable, he decided. Her grandfather had been her only human contact for so long . . . his heart reached out to her in sympathy.

As the days followed, they spent practically all the time together. They hunted, and he found that South Wind was as skilled as he expected. She competed good-naturedly, laughing at him when she bested him, but pleased, too, with his successes.

She was proving adept at her speaking skills, using new words, and occasionally asking for still more.

"How is that called?" she asked frequently, pointing to a circling hawk or a beaver playing in the pool.

She was amused at the name for the great owl. They were sitting on the ledge watching the sunset and listening to the night-sounds come alive, when the owl called from the timber downstream.

"How is it called?" she asked, pointing toward the sound.

"That is *Kookooskoos*," he told her.

She laughed, delighted.

"He calls his own name!" she cried.

"Yes, he does."

In a remarkably short time she could carry a simple conversation, and seemed quite pleased with her progress. Fox was constant in his praise, which also seemed to make her happy.

"It is good!" she cried aloud. "We could talk, even in the dark, without signs!"

That advantage had never occurred to him, but was very important to South Wind as a new discovery.

The best times of all for him were those when they had no urgent need to hunt, and she would impulsively decide to suggest something. She would take his hand, and like an eager child, lead him to the special places of her childhood play. They swam, as before, and lay in the sun to dry. She took him to a hidden clearing in the woods, where she played with makeshift dolls long ago. With a hushed awe, she showed him hidden crevices where great piles of moldering buffalo bones were heaped.

"Do you know the story of these?" he asked.

"Grandfather said there was a great slaughter of enemies," she said. "I did not understand."

He told her the story of the Blue Paints, and the alliance with the Head Splitters against a common enemy. Sometimes he augmented the words with hand-signs, or paused to answer her questions.

She showed him a little cave, too small to stand in, that had been her lodge in play. Actually, it was little more than an exposed pocket in the cliff's rough face.

"It seemed bigger, then," she laughed.

The most difficult trial for White Fox was physical contact. Though he wanted desperately to touch and hold the girl, he did not want to take advantage of her childlike trust. She seemed completely unaware of any implications of bodily contact. She readily held his hand when they walked together; she touched him with no apparent concern while swimming or in the close quarters of the cave. However, not since the night of her terror, when she had sought his embrace for protection, had there been such closeness. She had seemed a little embarrassed afterward, and he was unwilling to embarrass her further, or to drive her from him by unwanted advances. He would let her make any overtures at her own speed, he decided. Meanwhile, he was grateful for any chance contact, and for the impersonal hand-holding that came so naturally to her.

They grew closer to each other, both enjoying the companionship. It was easy to forget the reason for their odd life-style. It was almost possible for White Fox to think that the entire theory of the Evil Thing was in their imagination. South Wind seemed so happy with her newfound freedom, and showed such little concern, that he was beginning to develop a new plan. If there continued to be no further problem from the dark crevice, could they not assume that their indifference had weakened the Thing? Maybe ignoring it had weakened it, perhaps even killed it. Soon he would suggest his theory to South Wind, and ask her to leave with him. He was beginning to suspect that she would consent. He longed to take her to meet his mother and father. If he could only convince her that they had won the fight, that the Evil Thing was dead.

All of this came to an abrupt end one late afternoon. They had been swimming, laughing, and playing as they splashed like a couple of children. They lay on the sand, exhausted, and talked and laughed some more.

"I know!" South Wind said suddenly. "We will sleep down here tonight. Over there, on the other shore!"

White Fox smiled.

"Good! I will bring . . ."

"No," she said, laying a finger on his lips. "You stay here. I will bring our robes."

She jumped to her feet and shrugged into her tunic, then quickly leaped like a deer up the path. Fox watched her lithe agility with admiration. Surely there was never such a woman, he thought. He closed his eyes and lay dreamily in the sunlight. The shadows were lengthening, but it was still fully daylight. It would be a while until dark. They could build a little fire and spread their robes near it, and . . .

His pleasant fantasies were interrupted by the loud slap of a beaver's tail. There was no mistake; it was the warning slap, not that of play. It was followed by a scream. It was a loud and piercing scream from the cliff, unmistakably South Wind, and plainly a scream of terror.

Instantly he was on his feet, had grabbed his bow and arrows, and was running up the narrow cliff path. He passed Wind's child-hood play-lodge cave, and the wide place on the ledge where Grandfather lay. On and up, his legs aching and his lungs gasping for air. He rounded the last rocky shoulder before the cave, and almost collided with the girl. She was backing cautiously down the path, her eyes glued to the cave entrance.

"Wind! What is it? Are you all right?"

The girl turned and looked at his face for a moment, her expression a blank, dazed fear. She cringed against the wall of the cliff, and slowly bent her knees and slid down to a sitting position, her arms hugged around her legs. The dark eyes that stared at him were wide with terror. When she spoke, it was barely a whisper, but it was accompanied by rapid, fluttery hand-signs. That, he decided, was most chilling of all.

"I saw it," she signed. "I *saw* it! In the cave . . ."

His heart pounding from fear as well as exertion, White Fox stepped past her to the mouth of the cave. He fitted an arrow to the bowstring, thinking even as he did so how useless such an action would be. He looked inside, and there was nothing. Was South Wind going mad? Or was *he?*

Then, as his eyes adjusted to the dim light, there seemed to be a movement at the back of the cave. It could have been his imagina-tion, but he knew it was not. It was near the crevice, maybe partly *in* it, a formless dirty brown something, slithering along the floor to retreat into nothingness. He thought he could even hear the rustling sound as it receded. Then it was gone, and for a moment, he thought it had not existed at all.

But there was the faint odor of decay, like that of rotting vegetation in a stagnant pool. Had he noticed that the other night, or had South Wind only told him of it?

Trying to ignore his sweating palms, he stepped boldly inside and toward the back of the cave. He would rather have run. As deliberately as he could, and with a pretense of boldness, he stepped back. Not taking his eyes from the crevice, and trying to ignore the half-imagined slithering sounds from that dark hole, he backed away. With one hand he groped for the sleeping robes, tossing them over his shoulder, and backed slowly on out the doorway.

"Get up, South Wind," he said firmly. "Go on down. I am here."

Slowly she stood up.

"You are coming, too?"

"Yes, right behind you."

She hurried ahead, glancing back apprehensively from time to time. White Fox, too, looked behind him occasionally. He was badly shaken by the experience.

When they stepped onto the narrow strip of level ground next to the river, South Wind turned and flew into his arms. They stood there, the girl sobbing emotionally, and White Fox holding her close, trying to stop shaking, himself.

"It *was* there, wasn't it?" she kept repeating. "You saw it. It was there."

White Fox agreed, from time to time, because it seemed to reassure her. In his own mind, he was thinking rapidly. Yes, he had seen it. At least, he thought so. But there were other thoughts, too. This was the first time that even South Wind had seen the dark Thing in daylight. It was the first time he had seen it at all. Now they both had smelled it, too. Or had the damp smell of the cave made him imagine that? He was almost sure, also, that he had *heard* its slithering sound in the crevice.

South Wind finally calmed, and stepped back. Her big dark eyes looked directly into his.

"Something is wrong," she said quietly. "It is not weaker, it is *stronger!*"

That was it, what he had been afraid to admit, even to himself. The Evil Thing in the Rock was growing stronger.

# 20

## >> >> >>

They built a fire, and huddled together over it, sharing their robes. There was little sleep. The fire was much larger than necessary for warmth. Both seemed to want to drive the shadows back into the darkness. It was a fearsome feeling, not knowing what to expect. Each shadow, each familiar sound of the night creatures in their usual activities, was now transformed into a threatening, supernatural Thing.

*Kookooskoos* called downriver, and the hollow sound, in this new situation, caused them to cling to each other in dread for a moment. Sometimes they drifted almost into sleep, and then one of them would suddenly jump in alarm, wakening the other. Then they would build up the fire again, and huddle tightly together in their shared robes. The warmth and closeness gave them courage, gave them enough reassurance to survive the night of terror.

That night seemed endless, but finally morning came. Now they recalled that during that night they had seen no actual hint of the presence they dreaded, the Evil Thing. Maybe it was not yet strong enough to come out of the cave into the real world, even after dark.

It was much easier to think calmly and objectively with the sun shining through the leafy tent that stretched overhead. The bird songs of the morning seemed to make all the terrors of the night a bit foolish. White Fox had begun to doubt his own senses. Maybe, he thought as he gathered firewood along the river, maybe he hadn't actually seen the Thing. Maybe it was only in the girl's mind, her fear coming at him so strongly that he *thought* he saw, smelled, and heard things that were not there at all. But no sooner had he nearly convinced himself than he had to admit that it had been very real to him, too. The lasting impression of that dirty smudge of brownish mist in the crevice was real. Even if he had been able to reason that away, there was the warning that had come just before South Wind's scream. The tail-slap of his beaver spirit-guide had been unmistakable.

When he returned to the fire, he was already convinced, even before South Wind brought up the question. She approached it much as she had on the previous evening, though more rationally.

"Fox, this is not in my head? You *did* see it, too?"

White Fox paused for a moment before answering.

"It may be in your head," he observed, looking straight into her face, "but it is in mine, too."

She looked at him in serious concern.

"Are we both going crazy?"

"Maybe so, but I do not believe it. We have to get away from here or we cannot tell."

"But we cannot leave. You know, too, now!"

"Yes," White Fox agreed.

Unspoken between them was the thought that before last evening he could have gone. Now it was as impossible for him as for South Wind. Now, not only the girl, but White Fox, too. Both were burdened with the torment of the being in the crevice. Whether it was merely a creation of her imagination no longer

mattered. White Fox privately thought that something about the
weakening mind of the grandfather was involved. The creature
had seemed to feed and strengthen on the weakness of the old
man's mind. Whether the Thing had *caused* the grandfather's
madness, or had merely taken advantage of it, Fox did not know.
But, he felt that both he and South Wind were rational and sane.
They had experienced similar episodes which indicated that the
Evil One was becoming stronger. If it was only a thing of the
mind, it still involved them both. And, as he had reminded himself
before, it did not really matter. Whether it was a creature of this
world or the Spirit World, whether it was real or only in the minds
of the two of them, it must be dealt with. It seemed more certain
to him all the time that it must be dealt with here, at Medicine
Rock.

He was not quite certain how the confrontation might take
place. It would be good if he, White Fox, could take the initiative,
could speak the challenge. He did not know quite how to do that.
It was easy to challenge a friend to a contest at the hunt, or even
challenge an enemy to combat. There was something about the
possibility of challenging an unseen Thing which lived in a hole,
and which might even exist only in the minds of the two of them
. . . *aiee*, it seemed a little foolish. But he knew that it was not
foolish. Further, he believed that it would be much better to have
the coming confrontation as soon as possible. Since it appeared
that the Thing was growing stronger, then the sooner the better,
but how? He felt somehow that there would be a definite advantage in initiating the conflict himself, rather than waiting for their
adversary to confront them. That had already happened, last evening, and both he and South Wind had been too terrified to be
rational, much less meet the challenge.

No, they must devise a plan. He must ask South Wind to tell
him all that she could about the nature of the Thing in the crevice.
Then he must try to recall all that Looks Far had told him. The old
medicine man had stuffed so much information into him in so

short a time, had tried to teach him the plants and herbs to use, and had helped assemble the pack . . .

He paused, and a sharp inhalation of his breath caught the attention of South Wind.

"What is it?" she asked, alarmed.

"I . . . I . . ." he stammered, his face pale and his palms sweating. "The medicine bag . . . I left it in the cave!"

He had his doubts as to whether South Wind could possibly understand the critical nature of this error. Looks Far had considered the bag to be of extreme importance. The power of its medicine might be the only thing that could defeat the Evil Thing in the Rock. He rose from his seat by the fire.

"I will go and get it," South Wind said calmly as she rose.

"No!" he said firmly.

Somehow, he believed that the girl was more vulnerable than he, to the onslaught of the unknown. It had first appeared to her, in her childhood dreams. All its activity so far had seemed to relate to the girl. Its activity toward him seemed a trifle hesitant, a bit weaker than toward the girl. And again, it did not matter much whether it was really true, or whether they only perceived it so. Either way, he could not allow her to attempt to recover the bag. It was his fault that it was lost, anyway, he thought glumly.

"I left it," he said as calmly as he could. "I will get it."

White Fox would rather have done almost anything on earth than climb that path to the cave, but it must be done. Trying not to show his fears, he splashed across the riffle and started up the path. At least he had the advantage of bright daylight. The rays of the sun, halfway up the morning sky, would be slanting into the cave's mouth. He tried to ignore the fact that the last appearance of the Thing had been in daylight. Anyway, he reasoned, that was evening, with shadows growing longer. This was different, with Sun Boy racing toward the top of his daily run. Everything was much more favorable for his purposes now. Besides, he was forewarned . . .

He did not really believe any of it. He was terrified at the thought of stooping to enter the dim cave, his eyes unaccustomed to the shadows. Whatever stalked him in the dark could observe him and act before he was aware of what was happening. And what *would* happen? With all the fears, with all they had seen and heard and smelled, with all they had *felt*, he and South Wind had no idea of the nature of the Thing; only that it was evil beyond the imagination. He must retrieve his medicine bag, and then start to make some sort of plan. Yes, a plan of attack, that was the proper approach.

White Fox stepped past the corpse on the ledge, pausing to sign a greeting as he did so. He had fallen easily into that custom, because South Wind did so every time she passed up or down the trail. It had seemed to please her when he had followed her example, and now it seemed a logical thing to do.

He hurried on and up. Outside the cave he paused for a few moments, eyes tightly closed and covered with his hand to attempt to adjust to the dim light. His heart was pounding, palms sweating, as he mustered all his courage to step inside. He knew exactly where the medicine pouch lay, against the far wall and a little to his left. He would go straight to it, his eyes not leaving the crevice. By sheer will he would keep the Thing at bay, while he picked up the bag and retreated.

He did not know what he expected when he entered and opened his eyes, but it was nothing like this. The bag was not where it had been lying. It was directly in front of him, almost at his feet. Toward the back of the cave, as his eyes adjusted, he could still not be certain what he was seeing. That entire portion of the shelter seemed to be obscured by the same dirty fog or mist which he had seen before. He could dimly see the willow racks, lying crushed and broken. At the same time he noticed that his pack was lying as if it had been thrown or flung with great force. The thongs were loosened, and the carefully chosen packets which contained the plants of the medicine man's rituals were strewn across the floor. He was terrified now, almost too frightened to run. He must keep his nerve.

Very slowly, eyes fixed toward the dirty smudge, he began to pick up the packets and put them in the empty pack-bag. In the depths of the rock, where he knew the crevice would be if he could see it, there was a suggestion of the same slithering sound as before. In addition, there was an angry hiss, like that of a defensively coiled snake. White Fox felt that the brown-gray mist was crowding toward him, threatening. He grabbed one last bundle of herbs, turned, and ran.

He knew that he must try to make a plan, but he was certain that part of the contents of his medicine pack was still scattered over the floor of the cave. And the Thing had now taken possession of the cave.

# 21

## »» »» »»

**H**e was almost as far down the trail as Grandfather's burial ledge when he saw the figure ahead of him. The little man was sitting on a boulder. On South Wind's boulder, the one where she loved to sit and enjoy the pleasant evenings or bright cool mornings. That spot, near the wide place on the ledge, had been a favorite place for the girl during all of her childhood, she had told him. That was why she had chosen this for Grandfather's final resting place. Fox was a bit offended at the presence of another on the ledge. It should have been South Wind's, alone.

His predominant reaction, however, was fear. His knees were still shaking from the experience in the cave. Now, his head whirled in confusion, as he tried to appear calm and in control. That was not easy to do, when his instincts told him to run, and his reason told him that he was going crazy. But there was no place to run, and crazy though he might be, he was forced to confront this situation. At least, it was not as fearsome as the Thing in the cave. He stepped forward toward the boulder where the man sat, trying to show confidence where there was none. Could this be the spirit of the grandfather? he wondered.

"Greetings," he signed, "Are you the grandfather?"

The little man chuckled derisively.

"Of course not, stupid," he said, loudly and clearly.

White Fox thought that surely that would be the last of his sanity. This gnome-like little creature, hardly as tall as a man's waist, and in this improbable situation, had spoken to him in his own tongue.

"Who are you? How are you called?" White Fox blurted.

The little man did not answer, dismissing the questions with a wave of his hand.

"You are in trouble," he observed. "You and the girl, stupid!"

Anger rose in White Fox, bringing strength back into his legs. "But, I . . ."

"Be still, stupid," the little man interrupted. "Be still and listen. You may even learn something. Enough even, to save your skins!"

White Fox was no longer afraid, now. He was readjusting his thoughts and trying to remember everything he had ever heard about the Little People. He sat down, exhausted, and propped his back against the rocky wall of the cliff.

Nearly every tribe he had ever heard of, he recalled, had stories and legends of the Little People. In some, they were creatures who lived in water, sometimes coming out to do mischief. Some stories told of their protecting lost children. Sometimes the loss of small items that were misplaced or that disappeared unexpectedly was blamed on the mischief of the Little People. They could be helpful, or be an annoying nuisance, as they chose. White Fox had never really taken the stories of Little People seriously. They were tales told to children around story fires or in the long nights in winter camp. Certainly, he never expected to see one of them. He had never known anyone who had seen one of the Little People. Of course, there may have been a good reason. Anyone who told such an experience would be laughed at or considered crazy. There had been a visitor last year, from a faraway tribe, who talked of this. Among his people, the man had said, it was forbidden to tell of having seen one. A person who saw, and *told* of it, would die, immediately.

Since White Fox only half believed anyway, and certainly never expected to see such a being, he had never really wondered what they looked like. All of this was racing through his head as he looked at the droll little figure who sat on the boulder, nonchalantly swinging his feet. Aside from his short stature, the man appeared much as any other of the People. His hairstyle, his buckskin shirt and leggings, the breechclout, even the quillwork ornamentation on his shirt and his small moccasins were of familiar design.

"You do not really believe in us," accused the little man. "You are in trouble, I try to help, and still you do not believe."

He shook his head sadly.

"But I do!" blurted the confused White Fox. "I must! You are here."

"Are you sure?" taunted the man. "Really? Am I as real as that thing in the cave?"

"Yes, yes," agreed Fox eagerly. *"More* real. I can clearly see you."

Even as he said it, the outline of the little man's figure faded away, and White Fox found that he was looking *through* him.

"Wait! Don't go . . . come back!"

The outlines began to reappear, painfully slowly. White Fox watched, fascinated, while the little man once more assumed the appearance of flesh and blood.

"Ah, you *do* believe!" he said tauntingly. "Now, if you are not too stupid . . ."

White Fox bristled in anger.

"I . . ." he began.

The little man held up a hand to indicate silence.

"If you are wise," he advised, "you will be still now. If not, I leave you."

He seemed to wait a moment, and White Fox was quiet, so he nodded, a peculiar diagonal shake of the head.

"Now," he continued, "you have really mishandled this. You are so interested in getting the girl to bed that you do not think."

White Fox's ears burned with embarrassment. He wanted to retort, to deny it, but was afraid that the little man would disappear again. For reasons he could not have explained, he felt that he could not allow that to happen.

"You have almost ignored your Grandfather Beaver, your guide," the little man went on. "*Aiee*, Fox, you are stupid. You make it difficult . . ."

His voice trailed off in thought.

"Let me think . . . well, you lost part of your medicine . . . there is no help there. But, it can be done. Do you have a drum?"

"No."

"Then make one. But do it soon. That thing grows stronger."

"Yes, we have seen that. Can you tell me, what it will do?"

The little man cocked his head on one side with the peculiar little mannerism.

"Of course not. Only you know that. You and the girl. She gave it life, in her mind, and now it is in yours, too."

"It is not real?"

The little man threw back his head and laughed, a mocking laugh.

"Of course it is real, stupid. You have made it so. But it cannot do what you have not given it."

"But it has taken over the cave. It is stronger."

The little man nodded.

"Yes. You have made it so. You, and the girl especially . . . if you *think* it is stronger, it becomes so. Now you have given it the cave."

"What can we do? It *took* the cave!"

"Because you feared it would! *Aiee*, Fox, you make it difficult!"

"But now . . ."

"Well, make the drum. We will talk again. Do not tell the girl."

He started to fade.

"Wait!" cried Fox. "How are you called?"

"I am Fox, like you, of course. Small Fox."

He continued his disappearance.

"Do not tell the girl," he warned again, and was gone.

Bewildered, not even sure that the experience was real, White Fox moved on down the path. South Wind waited at the river.

"What happened?" she asked. "Did you get the pack?"

"Yes, most of it."

"Not all?"

"No. The cave is torn apart. But, I have a plan."

"What?"

"First, we must make a drum."

"A *drum?* What for?"

"I will show you, when the time comes."

There was no way he could tell her more, now, against the wishes of the Little Person who called himself Small Fox. She looked doubtfully at him.

"There is something else, Fox. I can tell. What is it?"

He shook his head.

"No, I will tell you later."

"I thought I heard you talking."

He nodded. This was a very uncomfortable situation. All his instincts cried out for him to share everything with this girl who had become the most important thing in his life. Still, he feared to tell her. What if the little man became angry at him and refused to help him? White Fox desperately needed his help. Maybe he could tell her everything later.

"Maybe I talk to myself," he told her. "I speak to your grandfather sometimes."

South Wind laughed.

"He cannot hear you. He is deaf, you know. But come, tell me about the drum."

# 22

>> >> >>

Of all the instruments created by man since the beginning of time, the drum has been most widely used. It expresses the deep desire to make sounds that have meaning. The beat of the surf, where the first air breathers crawled out to become land dwellers, is echoed in its cadence. It echoes the heartbeat of the first humans, and still gives meaning to the rhythm of ceremonies and pageantry in all cultures. Racial memory stirs at the drum's cadence; the feet become restless, and the listener begins to align his body rhythms to the motion of the dance. It is a primordial urge, the echo of the surf and of the heartbeat and of the first ritual dance steps of man in an attempt to create worship.

White Fox was not thinking along these lines, as he prepared to design his drum. It had been a reasonable suggestion. Many times he had watched Looks Far perform his ritual dances, in full costume and face paint. It was an impressive thing, to watch the old man chant the ancient prayers and dance the complicated maneuvers. And always, he was accompanied by his wife on the drum.

When he stopped to consider, he realized that they would have to create some sort of ceremony, and any dance or chant would necessarily be dependent on the rhythm of a drum. In fact, he was irritated at himself, that he had not realized the need and constructed a drum before this.

"We need a hollow tree or limb," he told South Wind. "Do you know of any?"

She led him to a cottonwood downstream, a giant which had stood against the ravages of sun, wind, and winter for generations. It was mature now, in the old age of a tree. It had been repeatedly blasted by real-fire when Rain-maker threw his spears and beat his own drums in the sky. The trunk was hollow, it could be seen, and woodpeckers and other small creatures had built their lodges in its limbs. Only a branch or two bore leaves now. Most of its great branches were the stark silvery-gray of the tree's dying.

"No, it is too big," White Fox said. "We need a smaller one."

"Tell me, Fox. I do not know. I have never seen a drum."

"Your grandfather . . ." he began.

Then he stopped. Of course, Grandfather was deaf. Still, it seemed that the man could have felt the vibrations of a drum's thump. Surely he would have kept a drum. But no, he would have been afraid that others would hear. Once more, the heart of White Fox felt sorrow for South Wind. Not only had she yet to see a drum, but she had never heard its beat or felt the exciting thump of its rhythm.

"Yes, I know," he said. "We will need a limb or branch about this round."

He indicated a circle a little more than a hand's span across.

"How long?" she asked.

"That does not matter much. Maybe like this."

He held his hands apart, again a span's width.

"It should have a hole through the middle, or nearly through."

Wind nodded, understanding now. She walked to a jumble of bushes a few steps away and pointed.

"Like this?"

Amid the tangle lay a large branch which had fallen from the main trunk of the cottonwood. Its weakness had been that which made it desirable for White Fox's purpose. It had broken through a hollow portion from its own weight. White Fox clambered over rocks and brush to reach the limb, which was nearly as large as his waist. But how far was it hollow? A stick, poked into the broken end, struck solid wood half an arm's length inside.

"Good!" he exclaimed. "This will do."

He climbed out to explain to her.

"I will cut it off, with the belt-ax. You take the pack, put the medicine-bundles out on a robe, and take the pack apart. Save the laces."

"Take it apart?"

"Yes. We need the rawhide for the drum."

She nodded, but did not start back to their camp. It took him a moment to realize that she was afraid to be alone so near the cave. He could understand that. He would feel much the same.

"I will go back with you," he offered. "We will bring the pack here. You can sit and work on it while I chop."

Her smile told him that this was the correct way to proceed. They went back to their makeshift camp at the river and retrieved the pack and a robe to hold the contents when it was emptied. Then they retraced their steps to the clearing with the giant cottonwood.

South Wind deftly cut the knot at the end of the lace and began to disassemble the pack. Fox drew his belt-ax and returned to the fallen limb. At a time such as this, he was glad to have the metal tools of the Spanish. *Aiee*, to think of trying to cut this limb with only a stone ax! There were some good things brought by the Hairfaces, even though it had meant problems for his mother's pueblo people.

He selected the proper spot and began to chop, very carefully, to avoid splitting the wood of the hollow shell. He was just fairly well started when South Wind came to tell him that she was finished with the pack.

"What should I do with it?"

"Find a good place to put it in the river. Weight it down with stones. The laces, too."

"To soften the rawhide!"

It was a statement, not a question, and she sounded pleased. Not to have reasoned about the rawhide, he suspected. That was simple. Her joy was in being able to put it into words. He smiled to himself. It was a pleasure to see her learn, to share in her delight at each new accomplishment.

It was nearly evening when the last cautious strokes of the little ax severed the limb. Triumphantly, he sheathed his ax and picked up the section of log. They carried it back to their camp, along with the partially softened rawhide and the robe with the plant bundles.

South Wind built up the fire and began to cook a rabbit. She had been hunting up and down the river during the afternoon. Now she placed the soaking rawhide back in the water, weighting it carefully.

Meanwhile, White Fox was studying his log. The hollow went almost all the way through, but not quite. He could see a darker area in the center of the fresh cut that suggested the beginning of decay. It was as he hoped, a good choice of a place to cut. His next move was to trim the splintered end of the log to make it straight and firm. This he did by slow and careful ax work, nibbling away the thin, split, or rotten portions. Sometimes he was able to prop his drum-log against a tree to support the impact of his ax strokes.

South Wind brought him meat, and he stopped long enough to eat, but he was feeling the urgency of the situation. He hated to go into another night without as much accomplished as possible. By dark, however, he had only smoothed the hollow end.

Again, the night was filled with fear. Without even mentioning it, they spread their robes together and shared warmth and drew courage from each other. The night-sounds, so fearsome and unearthly the night before, seemed less threatening now. Kookooskoos sounded his hunting call, but it did not have the ghostly quality of the night before. The green night heron called to his mate, but the odd cry did not suggest anything but normal sounds of the night.

For a long time after he heard the deep regular breathing of the girl's sleep, White Fox was awake, thinking. Again and again he visualized the next steps in the making of the drum. He had no idea what would come after that, but he had more confidence now. Whatever was ahead, there was now a semblance of a plan. And the little man had promised to return.

The sleeping girl stirred softly and cuddled closer. He cradled her gently, and lifted the corner of the robe over a bare arm. Yes, surely things were going better.

# 23

>> >> >>

**S**outh Wind watched as White Fox carefully centered the section of log. He had been working with it before nightfall, and was up at daylight to continue his task. She was not certain about this drum, or how it had a place in the plan he had devised.

Now, he had taken the largest piece of rawhide from the stream, and had set the log on it. With a partly burned stick he drew a circle around the log, keeping his charcoal line two or three fingers away from the wood.

"Here," he said, "you cut the circle from the skin. I will work on the log."

He built a very small fire, and found three flat stones to place around it. She saw that he had managed to make a small hole in the solid end of the log. Now there was the beginning of an opening all the way through the center. In fact, he explained, the shape inside was much like the inside of a lodge, with a smoke-hole at the top. He dipped the open, thin-walled end of the log in the stream and then set it on the stones over the little fire. There was much hissing and steaming, and soon a plume of smoke was spurting from the hole in the top end of the log. When it began to blaze, White Fox lifted the log and dipped it completely underwater to extinguish it. Then he sat down with the still steaming cylinder between his knees. Patiently, with his ax and his knife, he scraped and chipped away the charred wood, enlarging the hole. Then he set the log back over his fire, and tossed in a few twigs to repeat the process.

By noon, the log was hollow all the way through, and he was scraping and thinning the walls both inside and out. Then he took the circle of wet rawhide, and punched holes with his knife point around the edge, eight or ten of them. South Wind did not quite understand the purpose until he began to shake out the laces from the pack.

"Not long enough," Fox stated.

He cut the other pieces of rawhide into narrow strips, pulling, twisting, and rolling the resulting thongs. Then he started to assemble the drum, placing the rawhide circle on the ground and the hollow wooden shell on it. First he laced it loosely, crossing the center of the open end with each turn of the thongs. Once that was complete, he started around again, pulling each thong tighter, taking up slack as he went. Still one more time he retraced his motions, now drawing each turn tight. He turned the drum over, and thumped the skin experimentally with his finger.

"It makes no sound," the girl protested.

White Fox laughed.

"It must dry, first," he explained.

He set the drum near their campfire, and turned to another task. He cut a dogwood stem as long as his arm, and as thick as a finger. Gently, he began to bend one end of it, forming a loop about three fingers across, in the shape of an oval.

"Here, hold this while I tie it," he asked.

South Wind held the loop while Fox took scraps of rawhide from the pack and tied it firmly in the desired shape.

"There," he announced, "our drum-beater."

That afternoon and evening, the rawhide drumhead began to dry and shrink. Little creaking noises came from it as it drew tighter, stretching taut over the log. From time to time White Fox lifted the drum, tapped the stiffening rawhide, and turned a new segment to the warmth of the fire. The creaking noises continued.

During the night he rose from time to time to replenish the fire and turn the drum to warm a different side. Otherwise the night was uneventful. When morning came, he squatted on his heels before the fire, holding the drumhead to the heat to dry the dew from its surface.

Now he picked up the drumstick and began to tap tentatively on the hardened skin. To South Wind's astonishment, the soft, muffled thump that had come from the wet rawhide was now a pure and ringing tone. As Fox began a regular cadence, she felt a thrill of excitement. Like a child, she clapped her hands in joy, swaying and moving with the rhythm of the drum's thump.

"Here, you try it," he offered.

Eagerly, she took the stick, and began to tap experimentally. It was good. She quickly found that there was a difference in tone at the center and near the edge of the taut skin. Likewise, a firm blow produced quite a different effect from a light tap.

White Fox was dancing a few steps in time to her drum cadence.

"A little slower," he suggested. "Yes, that is better."

He showed her other things, how the drum could be used to accompany the Song of Fire, a prayer of thanks for the benefits of that great gift. There were other songs, the song of thanks for the return of the buffalo each season, the song of success in honor of a good hunt.

Ah, she thought, Grandfather had missed so much by his deafness. She wondered if he could ever, before their arrival at the Rock, feel the exciting thump of the drum through his skin and flesh. She could understand his reluctance to make noise, since they had hidden from all the world.

Somehow, that secrecy did not seem so important, now. She could hardly believe that she had contacted, and was living with, an outsider. Moreover, it was not frightening at all. It was comforting. She felt the protection of White Fox's presence, and a security that she had not felt since Grandfather's death.

Even with the Terror that lurked in the Rock, she felt a security in the presence of White Fox. And, of course, in his arms. There was another excitement in that, too, which she did not completely understand. The feeling was warm and good and exciting when she pressed her body against his in the sleeping robes. She must ask him more about that.

But just now, she was fascinated by the excitement of the drum. She had forgotten, almost, the danger of others who might overhear and come to investigate. White Fox would know how to deal with them, if anyone came. He had lived among other people all his life, and seemed none the worse for it. As much as she had loved her grandfather, she now began to suspect that there may have been something wrong with his thinking. She hated to admit, even to herself, that it might be true, but the facts were becoming undeniable. If all other people in the world thought differently from Grandfather, might it not be that *he* was wrong, and not everyone else? White Fox seemed so happy and proud, as he talked of his parents. She began to wonder about her own parents, and what sort of people they had been. It seemed a certainty that they were dead. Both Grandfather's brief and bitter tale, and the version remembered by White Fox suggested the same thing, that everyone had been killed except the two of them, the infant South Wind and her grandfather, half crazed with grief. He had saved her life, but at great sacrifice to them both.

"Fox," she said suddenly, as a new thought struck her, "do you think Grandfather was always deaf, or was he made that way by the day of the killing?"

"I do not know. The story . . . I am sorry, I just do not remember. We can ask some of the old people, who might have known him."

This came as a shock. It was the first time for many days that he had mentioned rejoining his tribe. *Their* tribe, it now seemed. It did not seem as great a threat as it once had.

But such thoughts ignored their first concern, the Thing in the Rock. They must deal with that. She lifted the drum.

"What do we do now?" she asked. "Is the drum ready?"

It bothered her a little that he did not seem to have a ready answer. In fact, he seemed a little devious, as if there might be something he did not want her to know.

"We will see," he said vaguely. "I will tell you later."

It was most unlike him, and she was a little angry at him. She wanted him to share all his thoughts and plans.

# 24

>> >> >>

**W**hite Fox had gone downstream to gather firewood. He had found himself back at the clearing with the old half-dead cotton-wood, picking up dead branches, when he heard the voice.

"*Ah-koh,*" said the small one.

Startled, Fox looked up to see him sitting on a limb overhead and swinging his feet.

"You are doing well," the little man observed sarcastically. "You have not done anything *too* stupid for nearly two days."

White Fox was infuriated by the condescending manner, but managed to control his anger.

"I have made the drum," he stated defiantly.

"Yes, it is so," agreed the other, with the odd, head-tilted man-nerism. "And, acceptably."

Then, he paused and seemed to change the subject.

"The girl handles the drum well," he observed. "Yes, maybe that . . . yes," he mused, half to himself, "that is it. She plays the beat; you sing. And dance, of course."

The gnome-like figure started to fade.

"Wait!" cried White Fox. "I do not understand."

"Of course you do! Make a song, a dance, use some of Looks Far's bundles. *Challenge* the cave!"

"What did you say?" asked a voice behind him.

Fox whirled. There stood South Wind, her arms filled with sticks, smiling happily at him. In a panic, he turned back to the tree. There sat the little man, chuckling at Fox's confusion.

"What are you looking at?" the girl asked, peering upward.

"I . . . I . . ." Fox stammered, unsure.

"Remember, she cannot see or hear me," taunted the small one. "Are you sure you want to tell her? She will think you are crazy."

"I . . . was looking at that limb," White Fox excused lamely. "It would make good firewood."

South Wind looked at him, puzzled.

"It is too big, and too green," she observed. "Besides, we could not reach it. Fox, is something wrong?"

"No, no!" he blurted.

The little man who called himself Small Fox was laughing hard now, tremendously enjoying this.

"*Aiee!*" he chortled, "you are so clever. She must really admire you now!"

Fox was unable to answer, and glared upward.

"White Fox, what is the matter? If we need that limb for your plan . . ."

The little man was rocking back and forth now, hugging himself in glee. White Fox was afraid he would fall, and wondered if he could be injured. He almost hoped . . .

"Ah!" exclaimed the little man, breathless, "ah, Fox, you may have to *find* a use for this limb to satisfy her."

He wiped the tears of laughter from his eyes.

"Tell her," he went on. "Tell her about the song and the dance, that she plays the drum while you sing and dance."

"About you?" Fox asked.

"What?" said South Wind.

*"Aiee!"* chortled the little man, laughing again. "You will talk yourself into trouble! Tell her if you want. She will only think you crazy!"

He faded suddenly and was gone.

"Wait!" exclaimed White Fox.

"What?" said South Wind again. "I am sorry, Fox. Sometimes I do not understand the word-sounds. Say them slower."

"Uh . . . wait," he repeated. "I said wait a little and we will go back to camp. I need a few more sticks."

There was a mocking chuckle from somewhere above, but he pretended not to notice, and South Wind apparently did not hear.

He picked up a few more sticks and they started back to camp. South Wind kept looking at him a little strangely, which made him a bit uneasy.

"I will tell you of the plan," he said finally. "You will use the drum, and I will dance and sing."

*"That* is the plan?"

"Yes, of course," he snapped, a little irritated.

"But I do not know . . . the drum . . . I have never . . ." she mumbled.

"But you have the touch, the rhythm," he protested. "We will practice. I must have a song . . ."

"You know it already?"

"No, I must make a song. You must help me!"

"I . . . I will try!"

"Good! We will start, right after we eat!"

The girl did, indeed, have a good sense of rhythm. In a short while her cadence was steady and strong. He sang softly, making words, trying one phrase, then another.

> Come out, Evil One, you
> are afraid to face me,
> You who frighten children
> in the dark . . .

He would pause, rearrange the words in his mind, and nod for South Wind to resume the drumbeat.

> Come out, cowardly frightener
> of little children, and
> face a man . . .

As the song took shape, he began to devise a few dance steps. He had watched Looks Far in ritual ceremonies, dancing with precise steps while his wife, Blue Dawn, tapped the drum. He had always been impressed by the exactness, the nonvarying cadence. Whether the steps were a shuffle or a quick stomping motion, the accuracy of each beat and the accompanying step now became of great importance. At least, he thought so. It seemed to him that the very precision, the predictability of the rhythm and the song, was his goal in this situation. The Thing in the rock was not a part of the normal world, but a freakish thing, a denial of the way of all things created. It did not follow the way of all things, but was an outlaw spirit. It could be controlled, then, by overwhelming it with the regularity of the drumbeat, the dance, and the song, to which it could not adapt.

At least, he devoutly hoped so. That, in itself, was part of the problem. This Thing had been created in the mind of a child, or in that of a grief-crazed old man, or both. Now it had also entered his own mind. It was quite important to believe that the Thing existed only there, that it was not loose in the world. If in their minds they could confine it to the cave, drive it back into the crevice, over-power it with the constant regularity and rhythm of the drum and dance, the plan would work.

But above all, they must both be confident of the plan. They must believe that it would work, that the dark Thing *could* be driven back, cornered in the crevice and destroyed by the combination of will, ceremony, the medicine of Looks Far, and the precise cadence of the song and drum. He must try to explain all this to South Wind, and engender her confidence. He could tell that her strength was growing, and that she felt better now about their ability to challenge the Thing. But, she must understand the danger that would result if either of them wavered. He wished his own confidence could be a little stronger.

The song was coming well, a repetitious chant that would lend itself well to the beat of the drum. South Wind was becoming quite proficient at that. They would use a soft beat at first, then increase the volume as the song rose to a climax. The chant of the song, however, was designed to come in a circle, so that it might be repeated again and again, as many times as need be.

Now, if he could find a way to incorporate the use of Looks Far's plants and paint. Yes, face paint, that would be good. He went to look at what supplies were left, and see what might have been destroyed in the cave.

# 25

>> >> >>

The girl watched, fascinated, as he mixed the paints and prepared to paint. Willow twigs, pounded at one end to separate the fibers and soften them, would be his brushes.

"It is like cleaning one's teeth?" she asked.

"No. The brushes are made the same way."

He held up the flattened tip of the willow twig.

"It could be used to clean teeth. I will use this one for paint."

He laid it aside and reached for another twig. He held it on a smooth stone and pounded it with a smaller one in his hand.

"Your grandfather never used paint?" he asked. "Face paint?"

"No." She shook her head. "Not any kind. What does it do?"

He hesitated. How to explain face paint to someone who has never seen it?

"It is a ceremonial thing. You know about Sun Boy?"

South Wind brightened.

"Yes! Grandfather told me! He carries the torch across the sky."

"Yes, it is good! Now, when he nears Earth's rim, he stops to paint himself, so he will be beautiful when he comes to his lodge. He uses many bright colors."

She nodded, but still appeared puzzled.

"But . . . you will make yourself beautiful, now?"

"No, no, this paint is for a different purpose. Look, first we will paint the drum."

Looks Far had suggested designs that would be appropriate, in reds and yellows and black. They were figures suggesting the natural order of things, the sun, moon, sky and earth, day and night.

"Your face paint must be your own designs," the old medicine man had said. "When the time comes, you will know."

White Fox was uncertain about that, but first, the drum. With his willow brushes of different widths, he began to decorate. The drum took on new spirit, a life of its own, as he worked. Even the sound of it seemed livelier, more intense and far-reaching. South Wind was enthralled.

"This gives the drum its spirit?" she asked.

He shook his head.

"No. It has had its spirit, since we made it. Before that, even. When it was growing, as a tree and as the buffalo whose skin we used. We brought them together."

"Then the paint? What did it do?"

"The paint gives beauty, and that gives pride to the spirit."

He tapped sharply with the stick.

"See? You can hear the pride of the drum. It is stronger."

The girl nodded.

"What now?"

He looked at the sun. The day was passing, too rapidly. He wanted to attempt the ceremony during the morning, while the sun was rising. It seemed to him that it was more appropriate to their purpose than afternoon. When the shadows were lengthening, the creatures of the night preparing to come awake . . . no, that would not be good. It would be approaching the time of greatest power of the things of darkness. The evil, dark Thing would be at its strongest. No, it would be best to wait until tomorrow.

Meanwhile, he would think about the patterns for his face. The designs would be similar to those on the drum, but would accentuate his own spirit. In his mind, he was drawing the stripes and broad bands, choosing the colors. He checked the gourds that contained his paints, making certain that there was enough. He went over the songs and chants that he intended to use. He hesitated to admit it, but he probably could have gone ahead that day. There would have been time, before Sun Boy stood overhead. White Fox knew that he could not show fear. Confidence was all-important. Therefore, he could not admit, even to himself, that he dreaded the coming confrontation.

Well, one has more confidence in the morning. So be it.

They rose with the dawn to begin preparations. The day was hot and still, and wisps of fog hung heavily along the river. White Fox had wakened early, and the tension of upcoming struggle kept him awake until dawn.

It seemed inappropriate, somehow, that birds sang and beavers splashed at play, considering the grim reality that lay before the two young people who camped at the Rock. South Wind watched intently as he knelt by a still pool and began to apply his face paint, using his reflection in the water as a guide. Stripes of red and yellow across the nose and cheekbones, broader bands on the forehead.

"It is good!" she observed. "You look very dangerous."

Finally, after much meticulous study and attention to minute details, Fox had to admit that he could postpone the event no longer. He stood up.

"It is time," he said, and noted that his voice sounded like that of a stranger.

South Wind nodded and picked up the drum. She tapped it softly.

"It does not ring, like last night."

"Warm it by the fire," he suggested. "The dew has softened it."

They waited impatiently while the drumhead dried to its former ringing tone. She tapped it again.

"Now, that is better!"

Together, they crossed the stream at the riffle, walked across the sandy beach where they had spent happy afternoons in the sun, and stood on the grass at the foot of the path. White Fox looked upward. His hands were restless and damp as he gripped the small pouch of plants provided by Looks Far. In his left hand, he held a small gourd rattle. He would use it in time with the cadence of the drum.

"Now," he said, trying to appear calmer and more confident than he actually was, "we will stop a little before we reach the cave. There we start the drum and the song. You know the song's beat, but listen to the rattle, too. It must be steady . . ."

"Yes, yes." She nodded, understanding.

"Stay behind me. When I go into the cave, you can stay at the door, or come in behind me. Whatever seems best."

She nodded again.

"I am ready," she whispered.

"Then let us go."

He turned and started up the path. They would be quiet until they were almost to the cave, and then use the element of surprise. It was pleasing, amusing almost, to think of the sudden effect of the drum and the song. Yes, anxious though they might be, White Fox had utmost confidence that their plan was a good one. They had planned well. Looks Far would be proud. This was the day of the final struggle, when South Wind would be free of the terror of the Evil Thing. It was good. Then, they could begin to build a life together, as she learned to live with the ways of the People. He could hardly wait to show her the people of his childhood. His parents, his friends, Looks Far . . . yes, most especially, Looks Far. They would sit with the medicine man and relate their triumph, and how they had, with his help, defeated the fear of the Thing.

They had passed the play-lodge of South Wind's childhood now, and were approaching the ledge where Grandfather lay. He must begin to be alert now. On up the trail, he must stop the daydreaming, and concentrate on the task at hand.

Now he was opposite the funeral-wrapped figure. From habit, and out of respect, he turned to nod a greeting. Then everything seemed to happen at once. He had no time to be very clear about it in his mind. There was the slap of the beaver's warning below, and he glanced down, which was a mistake. The motion, which he completely failed to anticipate, he saw only from the corner of his eye. It came from the little recess in the cliff's wall, behind the corpse. It was a formless, shapeless thing, like a dirty brown mist.

He had a fleeting impression that it was much more solid than before, and stronger. There was no question that it moved faster. It *lunged* at him, with an obscene hiss. He was uncertain whether it *pushed* at him physically, or whether his revulsion caused him to jump away. Either way, without a single beat from the drum or the rattle, without a word from the song, he found himself toppling over the edge of the path, and plummeting toward the river. He had barely time to note that this time, the fall would not end in the water as before, but on the rocky shore.

Above him, he heard the girl's terrified scream.

# 26

>> >> >>

The breath was knocked from his lungs as he struck, and he partially lost consciousness. There was no pain, at first. It was simply that he could not breathe. He struggled, gasping for life, splashing feebly in the shallow water. It seemed a very long time before his muscles relaxed enough to allow him to fill his lungs. His awareness began to return. He was lying partly in and partly out of the water. Somehow, he had missed the jumble of rocks that piled against the base of the cliff, and landed half on the muddy shore. He wondered if his spirit-guide . . . no matter, now. He was alive.

But close on that realization came another. He had failed. He looked up at the cliff's face, looming above him. At the top the sky was a bright blue, with puffy white clouds, drifting soundlessly like breath-feathers of some great white bird. By contrast, the dark stone of the Rock seemed to mock him. He had failed. He found that he had difficulty even trying to move. His thoughts were confused, dream-like. He seemed to have grown a third leg. At least, there was a foot, with a moccasin he recognized as his own, jutting at an improbable angle beside his waist. With alarm, he realized that his foot should not be there. His leg would not bend that way. It was not until then that the leg began to throb fearfully, and every fiber of his body began to hurt.

Through the pain, he heard South Wind calling his name from the cliff above. He wondered if she was safe. At least, she was alive. No one was safe, he thought now. The Thing had escaped the cave, and was coming down off the Rock. Would the world *ever* be the same?

He had failed. He should have tried to defeat it; he should have fled the Rock and its hideous terror and left it to die there, without escaping into the world. But he knew that would not have been successful. The Thing, born in the mind of the girl, would not have died until *she* did. Maybe not then, for it had entered *his* mind, too, and existed there. And he knew now, of course, that he could not have abandoned the girl to such a fate. South Wind had become more important to him than anything on earth. Except that, right now . . . his pain . . .

The sound of the girl's voice was coming down the path now. She had, at least, escaped the initial onslaught of the Thing. What was next, he dared not even think. His careful plan was destroyed, permanently.

"Well, you are not only stupid, but clumsy!"

The gnome-like figure of Small Fox was seated on the pile of jumbled rock, scarcely an arm's length away.

"*Aiee*, you make it difficult! I try to help you, try to tell you, the beaver warns you, and yet . . . *aiee*, what am I to do?"

White Fox was furious, angry, and in pain. He would have wreaked bodily harm on the little man if he could have reached him. If, of course, the small one had not disappeared.

"It was not easy," Small Fox continued, "to nudge you away from this rock pile."

He slapped one of the boulders with his hand.

"This would have killed you."

"It does not matter," White Fox said wearily. "It is finished. My leg . . ."

"Ah, yes," said the little man. "Your leg. Too bad. Now the girl will have to carry out the plan herself. Too bad. A good plan, too, if you had not been so . . . *aiee,* I must try to help a daydreamer."

He threw up his hands in resignation.

"Well, I hope she remembers to bring the drum," he finished, and started to fade.

"Wait!" White Fox almost shouted. "She cannot do this! She must not try to do it alone!"

The little man chuckled disdainfully.

"*Aiee,* you *are* slow, Fox! Do you not see, there is no other way? What could you do? And, there is surely no one else! I hope she remembers the drum."

The last seemed almost said to himself as he faded and was gone.

"Fox! I am coming!" called South Wind.

Her voice sounded from the bottom of the path, and he heard her splash into the water now. In a moment she appeared, wading, pausing to feel for her footing, calling encouragement to him. She stepped to his side and knelt, water running from her tunic in rivulets.

"Are you hurt badly?" she asked, and at the same time noticed the leg. "*Aiee!*"

"Where is the drum?" a voice asked from the pile of rocks.

White Fox looked, but saw nothing. Apparently South Wind did not even hear.

"Did you bring the drum?" he asked, through his pain.

"Of course! Fox, what . . ."

"Where is it?"

"On the bank, below the path. But, I . . ."

"Go and get it. Take it to the camp."

"Yes. But first I will help you."

"No. Now!" he insisted.

They must be sure the drum was not lost.

With apparent misgivings, she left him. He could see her cross the riffle with the precious drum, and disappear toward the camp. Soon she returned, crossed again, and waded back to him.

"Now I will take you across," she told him. "You must lie still and let me pull you."

"Yes," he agreed, "but first, you must pull my leg straight."

Together, they planned that procedure. She cut sticks to use as splints, and brought them to where he lay. Carefully, she cut away the legging from the injured limb.

"Cut it in strips to tie the sticks," he suggested. "Is the bone sticking through the skin?"

"No," she answered, "it presses, but does not break through."

"Good. Now, this will hurt, but you must do it, all at once, suddenly. Give me a stick."

He placed a length of willow as thick as his thumb between his teeth, to bite on against the pain.

"Now," he said, nodding.

He had known it would hurt, but was not prepared for the grating, grinding pain of the broken ends of bone as she pulled the leg into position. He would have screamed, except for the stick in his mouth. As it was, he nearly lost consciousness. He knew that the girl was strong, but he wondered if she would be able to pull against the big muscles of his leg with enough power to align it properly. There was a moment when he was in almost a dream state, and thought he saw a small gnome-like figure helping her pull.

When the leg was in proper position, it felt better. Not good, but better. She began to bind the splints in place, which gave him a great deal more confidence. It would help to guard against any chance motion.

Finally they were ready to cross the stream.

"Lie still," she told him. "Let me pull you."

It was hard to do, to float on his back without moving, while she made her way across, towing him by the neck of his buckskin shirt.

The injured leg trailed behind, painful but not impossibly so. She reached the bank, and he was able to help pull himself up on the shore.

"Now," she said, "can you stand and lean on me?"

"Make camp here," said the little gnome-voice which was becoming familiar. "You can watch the Rock from here."

Again, the girl seemed to hear nothing.

"Move the camp here," White Fox suggested. "That way we can watch the Rock."

"Yes, of course," South Wind said, rising. "I will bring everything back here."

She hurried away.

"*Aiee!*" exclaimed the little man's voice from the leafy canopy of a sycamore overhead. "You are claiming that idea, and it was mine!"

# 27

**》》 》》 》》**

**R**ed Feather sat with his back against the willow rest, watching the clouds slide quietly across the blue dome overhead. It was a day when he should have been enjoying the uncommonly fine weather, but he could not.

Moonflower looked out of the lodge for a moment, then went back inside without speaking. Red Feather knew that she, too, was troubled. Their son had been gone for nearly a moon. It was a strange thing, how White Fox had come home from his vision-quest. He had seemed much preoccupied, and had gone to talk to old Looks Far. After being at home only one night, he had rushed off again. It was something unusual that had happened on his quest, he had explained, that required him to go back.

"How long will you be gone?" Moonflower had asked.

"I do not know, Mother. Do not worry. Looks Far will know where I am."

After spending an entire day in active consultation with Looks Far, White Fox was gone.

Red Feather had become increasingly concerned for several days, now. He had said nothing to Moonflower, but he knew that she was concerned, too. She had always had an intuitive sense for trouble, especially illness or injury. That, in fact, was how they had met. *Aiee*, he had been younger than White Fox . . . but that was long ago.

The door flap lifted again, and Moonflower stooped to come outside. Red Feather watched her as she stepped toward him. She was still beautiful, even after many winters. He started to speak, but she held up a hand to silence him.

"I know. You are worried, too, about Fox. Red Feather, what is his mission?"

Red Feather shrugged.

"He did not tell me."

"Is there some custom that I do not know?" she asked. Her pueblo customs had not prepared her for some of the ways of the People.

"Probably," he smiled. "But not in this. There is some special need that caused him to go. He and Looks Far planned it."

He paused a moment, and studied her faraway look.

"You think he is in trouble."

It was a statement, not a question. She shifted her gaze from the far horizon to her husband's face, and looked deep into his eyes.

"Yes," she said softly. "Fox is hurt. I know you feel it, too."

"That he is in trouble, yes," his father answered. "Not that he is hurt. Do you really think so?"

She nodded. "Hurt, or sick. I do not know. We must do something."

"But what?"

"Whatever we must. Let us go and talk to Looks Far."

The medicine man did not seem surprised to see them. He nodded a greeting and then sat smoking for a moment, not speaking.

"Uncle," began Red Feather, "we are . . ."

"Yes, you worry about him, too," the old man commented.

"It has been a moon since he went away," explained Red Feather. "His mother and I . . . Uncle, could you tell us of his quest?"

The old man looked from one to the other.

"Only a little," he said sympathetically. "There was a woman, a young woman, there where he took his quest at the Rock. She appears to be in danger. Your son went to help her."

"What sort of danger?" Moonflower demanded.

"I am not sure," Looks Far pondered. "But, the past day, I have felt . . . well, you felt it, too."

"Yes," Red Feather answered, "his mother thinks that he is hurt."

The medicine man nodded.

"This does not surprise me," he said, directly to Moonflower. "Daughter, you . . . well, never mind."

He had been about to suggest that her sensitivity might lend itself well to a further study of his profession. Her tribe was known for its skills in matters of the Spirit World. But this was no time to suggest such a thing.

"Let me cast the bones," he suggested instead.

Blue Dawn brought a wrapped bundle and handed it to him. She had been her husband's assistant for so long, that it seemed she was a part of his skill. Looks Far unrolled the skin to reveal the painted surface used for this ceremony. Carefully, he spread it, rotating it until it pointed just so, the geometric designs aligned to their proper directions.

"It could be done more carefully at night, by the Real-star," he said apologetically, "but this will be close."

Now he took the cylindrical rawhide box that held the objects used in the toss. He shook it like a rattle, held it between his hands and then gave a sudden sweeping motion over the painted skin. Small bits of wood, bone, and stones skittered across the surface and came to rest.

"Ah, yes," he murmured, scanning the assortment. "Yes . . ."

He pointed here and there, mumbling to himself and nodding occasionally.

"What is it?" asked Red Feather, when he could stand the suspense no longer.

"I am made to think he is alive," the old man pondered, "but in trouble."

"Yes, go on," urged Moonflower.

"He has help . . . but . . . he is trapped, somehow."

"He cannot get away?" Moonflower asked.

Red Feather was thinking. He had much faith in the skill of Looks Far, but the medicine man had suggested nothing much that was new. Of course their son could not get away. If he could, he would come home.

"Uncle," he said respectfully, "could someone go to help him?"

The old man looked at him sharply, then studied the objects on the skin again.

"Maybe. He must handle his own problem. Yes, the danger, too. But it might be possible to help him. Yes, I think so!"

"Then, I could take a search party to look for him? We could do this without hurting his quest?" Red Feather asked.

"I think it would do no harm," Looks Far said agreeably.

"Good. I will start today. Do you know where he went?"

"Of course. Back to Medicine Rock. Where we killed the Blue Paints."

"Does this have to do with *them?*" asked Red Feather.

"No, no, only the same place."

"I am going with you," stated Moonflower.

"Can you ride?" her husband asked, astonished.

"As well as you!"

Well, she had always been a determined woman. For a girl whose people had little use for the horse, she had learned rapidly when he had brought her home to the People. She had quickly become an excellent rider, and had ridden as recently as their last trading venture to Santa Fe, five, no six summers ago. Yes, she could do it, Red Feather decided.

"I would go with you," Looks Far said apologetically, "but my bones have seen many winters, and move slowly. You will want to hurry."

Red Feather wondered if the medicine man intended to *advise* them to hurry. He decided not. Looks Far only wished to avoid becoming an extra burden for them.

"We will leave as soon as I can find men to go," Red Feather told him. "We will ask his brother, some friends. Maybe five or six?"

"Maybe. No more. Maybe only two or three. The danger is not of that kind."

What an odd statement, thought Red Feather. If not a danger of that kind, then *what* kind? Looks Far was plainly saying that force would not be necessary. Only a few men. Then it must be that this danger was a thing of the spirit.

It would be a great advantage to have the skills of Looks Far with them, but it did not seem practical.

"Do you have any advice for us, Uncle?" he asked.

Looks Far shook his head slowly.

"I tried to teach him what I could. He is a thoughtful young man. That will help."

They hurried away, Moonflower to assemble a few supplies, while Red Feather recruited the search party. Even that took a frustrating length of time. Some of those he sought were away on a hunt, one was thought to be courting, another off somewhere looking for a lost horse. It was nearly dark before they were ready to start. With them would be only two warriors, friends of White Fox.

"It will be no problem to travel," observed Moonflower. "There will be a full moon."

Red Feather was pleased that she was going with him. He had great faith in her feel for things of the spirit. And surely, this mysterious danger must be such a thing.

# 28

>> >> >>

South Wind gathered up their few scattered possessions. Their sleeping robes, weapons, what remained of the paints. It would require two trips, she noted. Maybe three, because it would be easier to carry coals for the fire than to start a new one.

She had been terribly frightened there on the ledge. It had all happened so fast. She had been only a step or two behind White Fox, dreading the confrontation but knowing that she must help him. They had come to Grandfather's resting place, and she was looking ahead, past Fox's figure. She always seemed to gain a little strength from speaking to the still form on the ledge.

It was then that it happened. The formless Thing had *jumped* at him. She could still hear the horrible hissing noise it made. She thought it pushed him, but maybe not. Maybe it was his involuntary jump that carried him over the edge. There was no chance to help him.

She had been rooted to the spot, expecting the Thing to attack her, next. But it had turned, if a formless thing may be said to turn. It changed direction, then, and retreated back up the trail toward the cave. Its motion was as indistinct as its form, like watching a snake as it flows silently into the grass. One moment you see the slowly sliding body of the snake, and then, while you still watch, it is gone. The Thing was that way. She had clearly seen the motion, sliding back up the trail. The motion was easier to see than the form or substance, which was still only the chilling something, half seen, the dirty brown mist that clung to the rock. Then it was gone.

She turned and ran, a terrible mixture of emotion gripping her. Much as she feared for her own safety, her concern for White Fox was even more. He could be dead or dying below. She reached the bottom and dropped the drum, to splash into the stream. She could not see him yet, but knew where he must have struck, on or near the pile of rock. She had dreaded what she would find.

She took a deep breath now, and returned to the task at hand. White Fox was alive. She would care for him until his leg healed and he could continue with his plan to defeat the Thing. South Wind had no experience with broken legs, but he had assured her it would heal.

She bundled an assortment of small items in one of the robes and carried it back to where he lay. He appeared to be doing well, though in some pain. She smiled and touched his face gently, then turned back toward the camp. It was not until the third trip that she brought the smoking and partly burned sticks to start the new fire. When it blazed up, coaxed by gently blowing and dry tinder, she felt better. There was a good feeling about a camp fire.

Now, she would go hunting for meat. She made him comfortable on his robe, picked up her bow, and started downriver to hunt.

It was well past midday when she returned, carrying a turkey. In a short while it was roasting, and for the first time since the accident, there was a time to talk.

"It was coming down," she noted.

"Yes."

"What will happen now?"

"I do not know. Did it come on down?"

"Not yet. It went back toward the cave."

"It was in full sunlight," he said, in a tone of unbelief.

"Yes, I saw it. Did it *push* you?"

"Maybe. Or, I fell. It does not matter."

"Maybe it does," she said thoughtfully. "We do not know what it *can* do."

It almost appeared that he shuddered. He seemed so helpless, lying there. She had gained so much strength from him, in the short time they had been together. She had almost come to regard him as invincible. Now, here he lay, defenseless.

"How long does it take a leg to become strong?" she asked, struggling a little with the words, and finally resorting to hand-signs.

"Two, maybe three moons," he suggested.

She was shocked.

"We cannot wait that long!"

"That is true. That is why *you* must do it."

"Do what?" she asked, alarmed.

"The dance, the chant. Oh, did you find the rattle?"

She ignored the question.

"No, Fox, I could not do that."

She felt dizzy and her head swam.

"I will help you," he offered.

She glanced at his injured leg, and saw an expression of hurt and shame cross his face.

"I know," she said gently, "but I could not do it. You must think of something else."

She rose and turned the turkey to brown on the other side.

"South Wind," he said seriously, "you *must* do this. There is no one else. You saw that the Thing is coming down."

"But I have never sung, never danced. How could I . . . no, Fox, I am afraid."

"I am afraid, too," he admitted. "I was afraid, this morning. But I was more afraid *not* to go."

"What do you mean?" she asked suspiciously.

"Listen," he pleaded. "First it was only in the crevice, in the dark. Then, it grew stronger and came out in the cave. We both saw it, and it showed itself in daylight."

She nodded. She was afraid that she understood.

"Now it comes down," he continued. "First only at night, maybe. Now, in sunlight. Do you not see? We *have* to stop it. It will come here, and we have decided that we cannot leave. It would follow us."

"Yes," she agreed, slowly. "Fox, do you think it can cross water?"

He did not answer for a moment. Then he spoke hopelessly.

"I think it can do anything *we* think it can do," he suggested. "Do you see why we must stop it?"

"Of course!" she snapped angrily. "I know we must do it, but *I* cannot. You must think of something else!"

"Wind, there *is* nothing. There must be a ceremony, and I am unable to do the dance."

A fearful thought occurred to her. What if . . .

"Fox, what if it . . . maybe it could have killed us anytime! Maybe it only plays with us. You know, a coyote catches a rabbit, then plays with it, lets it almost escape, but catches it again!"

"But that is for a purpose," he argued. "The coyote does that to teach her young to hunt."

He may have intended for that to be a reassurance. She saw, even as he spoke it, that he was sorry for his words, for the effect was anything but reassuring. She fought back the panic.

"Fox," she whispered, "do you think it has *young?*"

They stared at each other in horror for a moment, and she thought of something he had said earlier. "It can do anything we *think* it can."

"No!" She cried. "It is not true!"
But she realized that the thought had already occurred.
"This is why you *have* to do it!" he urged.
She shuddered.
"No!" she said firmly. "I will not. It is a thing I cannot do."

# 29

>> >> >>

"**S**he *must* do it," insisted the little man, in what was practically a shriek. "You must talk to her."

"I have tried," snapped White Fox. "She will not do it."

"But I can help her."

"Then you tell her. You know so much. Appear to *her!*"

The small one spread his hands in frustration, and cocked his head to the side.

"Fox, you do not understand. It is not that way. I appear only to you."

"Then someone else does, to her. Let him do it."

The other shook his round little head.

"No, it is not . . . I do not even know whether anyone . . . *aiee*, why do I have *you* to deal with?"

South Wind was downstream gathering firewood. They had not discussed their problem since her flat refusal. He had tried to approach the subject several times, but was met with a cold stare and a shake of the head. He had finally given up. He could do nothing physically, and she refused to talk.

He knew that she was concerned. Without saying anything to him, she had crossed the riffle, late in the afternoon, to build a fire on the path. Her purpose was apparent. It was an effort to prevent the Thing from descending all the way down. They had noticed, while they were still in the cave, that when they built up the fire, the Thing seemed to retreat. Well, he thought, maybe she is right. Maybe fire *is* the answer.

In his heart, he knew better. South Wind's fire, at a narrow place partway up, might stop further descent. But, it must constantly be replenished. She had risen three times during the night to build it up again, and had used up all their available wood. That, in fact, was why she had ventured farther away this morning.

He looked across at the cliff's face, where a thin column of smoke marked the girl's fire, her desperate effort to keep the Thing from escaping. She could not keep up the fire forever. Eventually it would go out, and . . .

"That fire will not keep it prisoner," the little man observed.

He was sitting on a knobby sycamore root. White Fox was always frustrated that the small one could read his thoughts.

"I know," he said. "The fire will go out sometime."

"And, there are probably a hundred other ways down the Rock," the little man commented, to no one in particular.

White Fox had not thought of that, but it seemed obvious now. Something with no shape or form, which seemed to be only a mist, might behave as a mist. It could be as thin as a morning fog, hanging over still pools along the river, or as dense as smoke. What was to prevent it from pouring over the ledge and sliding down the wall of the cliff? And he wished, for the hundredth time, that he had not mentioned the coyote teaching her pups. That thought had not been mentioned again, but he knew. South Wind was convinced that the Thing had young, somewhere in the dark recesses of the Rock.

That concerned him greatly. Increasingly, he had come to think that the Thing was able to take on whatever characteristics they might chance to think of. They had thought of its coming out into the cave, then *out* of the cave, now down the Rock. Had it done all these things . . . yes, the daylight, too . . . *because* one of them had first thought of it? That made the thought about the coyote's young one that he wished he had not had.

He was still convinced that his plan had been good. The chant and the dance *would* have been successful, except for the unexpected encounter. South Wind *could* carry out the plan, if she would, but she was terrified at the thought of failure. That was entirely the wrong approach. If, as he now suspected, the creature could take on any characteristic that appeared in their minds, that provided a way for it to grow stronger. He looked at the gnome-like figure, sitting dejected on the sycamore root.

"Tell me," White Fox requested, "is it true that the Thing in the Rock can do whatever we *think* it can?"

The little man spread his hands in the gesture of resignation that was becoming so frustrating.

"*Aiee!*" he cried. "Do you want me to give you all the answers?"

"But you said you would help me!" White Fox answered angrily.

"Help, yes. But I cannot *think* for you! I am going now. Try not to be stupid."

In the space of a heartbeat, he was gone.

White Fox lay there, fuming in frustration. His leg ached. He could do nothing to help himself, or to plan the defeat of the Evil Thing. South Wind was gone, gathering wood for her silly fire, to try to hold the Thing from escaping. It was amazing that by this time it had *not* come down from the Rock, and crossed the river.

He paused. He must *not* think these thoughts. That in itself might give the creature strength and ability to . . . there had been in his mind the picture of the dirty brown fog pouring over the ledge and down the rocky wall. What was that, high on the ledge? A misshapen wisp of brown that trailed over the rim . . . *No!* he cried silently. *I will not think these things!*

Sweat was standing on his forehead as he concentrated on *not* thinking that what he saw was real. It was much more difficult to think this way. If he could . . . slowly the answer began to dawn.

All of the characteristics of the Thing were from their minds . . . South Wind's, the grandfather's, and now, his own. If it could grow stronger through their thoughts, it could also grow weaker. They could place limits . . .

He focused his gaze on the wispy rag of brown mist that was spilling over the ledge. *But it cannot do that,* he thought. *It must use the path as we would.* The brown wisp hesitated a moment. A curl that had the appearance of a groping tentacle withdrew slightly, back into the shapeless glob.

"It is true!" he said aloud. "We can do it."

He imagined that he could hear a defensive hiss from the cliff, as the dirty brown scrap of mist pulled slowly up and out of sight. He was elated. He had found the answer.

This discovery also explained South Wind's success with the fire. She had decided firmly that her fire on the ledge would contain and imprison the Thing, and so it had. On the other hand, if she was now, somewhere downriver, thinking that it had young in the Rock . . .

He tried to remain calm. If she thought that, he must try to . . .

*It is not able to reproduce!* he thought. *It is not!*

Maybe if he said it aloud.

"You are limited. Evil One," he intoned. "Your power is weakening. You are thinner, weaker!"

This time he was sure he heard the hissing sound from the Rock. Now, if only he could tell South Wind the secret he had discovered. But she was far away. Probably, he feared, she was thinking of the Thing, too, but she was thinking of its growing stronger. *Aiee,* could he overcome this?

The drum, he thought. Yes, the drum. If he could sing and relate in a chant all the limits he could place on it, maybe he could overcome it. The drum lay a few steps away. A few steps. Under usual circumstances, it would have been no problem, but now . . .

he must have the drum! He lay back flat on the ground, and rolled over on his belly. It sent a sharp stab of pain through his injured leg, and he was forced to wait a moment for it to subside. Then he began to pull himself forward on his elbows, pushing with his one good knee. Around the fire, toward the drum. He paused to rest a moment, and looked back at the cliff.

He could visualize, now that he had become familiar with it, where the ledge ran which formed the narrow trail. Quickly, he scanned its wandering length. There, in at least three separate areas, tiny wisps of dirty brown fog were sliding over the rim of the ledge.

"No!" he yelled at the top of his lungs. "South Wind! It is not true! It cannot have young unless we let it!"

He struggled on toward the drum. He grasped it and sat up . . . where was the beater? There, a step away. He reached to grasp it, and started his rhythmic beat.

"You are helpless, Evil Thing!" he chanted. "You have no young. You are one alone. You fear the fire! You cannot stand against me . . ."

The dirty wisps seemed to hesitate and then to pull back. He paused for breath, and they slid forward again. Frantically, he resumed the chant. How long could he keep it up?

Shadows were beginning to lengthen . . . where was South Wind? Could she . . . no, he would not think that!

# 30

》 》 》

**S**he was deeply troubled, as she gathered wood that afternoon. When she was a child, and Grandfather had scolded or reprimanded for some misdeed, she had gone to one of her secret places to cry and be alone until she felt better.

It was like that now, except that she had cried very little, and she did not feel better. She was certain that it was not whether she cried or not. Her concern, and her heaviness of heart, was the feeling that somehow she had betrayed the trust of White Fox. She had seen the disappointment, the helplessness in his eyes.

She was deeply grateful to him. He had saved her sanity, perhaps her very life, since he had joined her at the Rock. His presence was strengthening, reassuring. He had become the most important event in her life. It was like having all the most comforting characteristics of her grandfather back again. Before his mind failed, of course. But in addition, the excitement of White Fox's closeness, the pleasure in his touch, was something she had never experienced before. The time since White Fox came to the Rock had been happy, at times even carefree. Except for the dreadful fear of the Thing in the Rock.

That was why he had come, it seemed, to help her overcome that danger. It was a bittersweet thought that it was also the thing which had driven them apart. She had refused to take the major part in the confrontation with the Evil One, and this had made him angry. No, not angry. He was hurt, and disappointed, and that in turn had made her feel the hurt. What was she to do?

There was no way that she could explain, either in hand-signs or in her newfound use of words, how she felt about it. Her very flesh crawled at the thought of that horror in the crevice. She had been right as a child. It *had* been there, despite her grandfather's comforting denials. That had been proved.

And now, it was out, free of the confines of the crevice, the cave, even. It had grown so powerful that she was afraid it could not be stopped. For a little while, she had believed that the two of them together, she and White Fox, could stop it, but now . . . he lay back at their camp on the shore, helpless, his leg shattered. He had asked her help, and she had refused, and her heart was heavy.

Her idea of the fire had been good. There was no doubt of that. It had been apparent that it had held the Thing at bay. But she knew that that was only a temporary obstacle. It could learn to come around, or over, or wait until the fire died down, to descend the path, and then . . .

She did not know what, then. She still had no real idea what the Thing might *do*, out of control, free of the confines of the cave. Certainly it had leaped, or lunged, at White Fox. That had been unexpected, had taken place when he was completely off guard, and the tragic fall had resulted. They must *not* be caught off guard.

With this main thought in her mind, she gathered wood. The maintenance of the fire had become the most important duty in her life. More important, even, than food. She could not see past today, and the day was devoted to gathering fuel. In the strange, hopeless existence that had now become hers, only one thing was certain. She must maintain the fire. It was necessary, to survive.

She had gathered and piled armfuls of wood, preparing to carry it back to the camp. Now she must do so. There was barely time for two trips, because Sun Boy was drawing near Earth's rim. She picked up one of the piles of sticks, which filled her arms. Maybe she could add one more . . . yes, that cedar branch, with the big knot where it had broken away from the trunk. The resin which oozed from that knot would burn long and brightly. With some difficulty, she knelt to pick up the cedar knot, and added it to her burden. She glanced again at the lowering sun. There might not be time for another trip. She must hurry.

She was nearly halfway back to the camp when she heard the rhythmic sound, and stopped to listen. Yes, unmistakably, it was the beat of the drum. She could hear the voice of White Fox, now, rising and falling to the cadence. What was he doing? There was an urgency to the chant and to the beat. He was not merely practicing his ritual. He would be unable to move, so could not be trying to go up the cliff path. There was only one other possibility, one that struck fear to her heart, but drove her feet into motion. The Thing had come down the cliff, and he was in danger. His drum-song was his only defense . . . his last defense.

She was running, now, still holding her precious load of fuel. There was no thought of dropping it, because it could be critical. There was a pause in the song, and she thought she heard him call her name. Her breath was coming in gasps now, and her knees were becoming weaker, but she must go on. She could not fail the man who had come to help her.

She plunged through the last thin screen of willows and saw their camp ahead, under the sycamore. White Fox was sitting with his injured leg extended before him. He held the drum, and his rhythmic beat echoed from the face of the cliff. He was looking upward, and her gaze followed his. There, at several points along the narrow trail, she could see the brownish wisps trailing over the edge, to slide downward. Instinctively, she looked toward her fire on the ledge. It still smoldered, and at no point did it appear that the dirty brown mist had *passed* that point. The fire still held the Thing at bay, and it must go around.

She ran forward, dropped her load of wood, and thrust the cedar knot into the campfire. White Fox paused a moment in his song, but continued the rhythmic drum cadence.

"Wind," he gasped, "it can do only what we let it. We must think and sing what it *cannot* do."

"It cannot cross fire!" she cried.

"Yes! And it cannot have young."

Then what . . . she thought, staring at the several wisps of brown fog.

"You cannot bear young," White Fox sang. "You are but scraps of the same Evil Thing!"

She saw the tendrils hesitate and recoil, and she began to understand. The two of them could deny the Thing's abilities. She had done it already with the fire. She was frightened, terrified, even, but could see that it *could* be done. Not by fearful waiting, thinking of every bad threat from the Evil One, but by denying its strength. She could do it. She must, for her own safety as well as that of White Fox.

His voice was growing hoarse. She did not know how long he might have been struggling to hold the brown mist from sliding over the edge.

She knelt and picked up the burning cedar brand, and spoke to White Fox.

"I do not have good words," she said apologetically. "You beat the drum, sing, if you can."

He started to protest, but she had already turned toward the riffle.

*You fear the fire, Evil One*, she thought. *You will fear me even more!*

She felt a strange exhilaration, an excitement, as she splashed across and stepped out on the other shore. Her stride began to match the cadence of the drum. Along the sandy beach, up the path, her torch carried high before her.

Behind her, White Fox had resumed his steady drum cadence.

*My fire will destroy you,* she thought. *You cannot stand against me!*

Her fire, the barrier that marked her success, was ahead of her now, on the ledge. It had burned low, but still served its purpose. Beyond it on the trail, she could see scattered scraps of the dirty fog. She must concentrate on the fire, and its effectiveness. It was growing dark rapidly now. This must be completed before darkness fell, or . . . no, that was wrong.

*You cannot come down,* she thought in a challenge that was almost a shout. *You are a captive here. I have held you on the Rock.*

She took a deep breath and stepped forward to kick her fire over the edge of the path. The partly burned sticks fell, and she heard them hiss into the water below. There was an answering hiss from the ledge, and a lunge forward from a dirty brown glob. She thrust at it with her firebrand and it retreated slightly. Trying to appear as confident as possible, she stepped over her scattered fire, swinging her torch in an arc before her.

"Back!" she shouted aloud. *Evil Thing of darkness. You cannot stand against the fire. Back, into your place of darkness!*

Despite her show of confidence, however, she could not fail to note that night was falling, and that the whole world would soon be in darkness. How long would the torch last?

# 31

>> >> >>

Step by step, painfully, slowly, South Wind moved up the familiar path. Her determination would waver a little, and there would be a sudden lunge at her from the rolling misty Thing as it retreated. She would thrust at it with her torch and it would retreat again.

Small scraps of dirty brown drew together from tiny hiding places in cracks and crevices, combining again with the main body. It was retreating faster now, rolling back up the trail ahead of her. She pursued it, aggressive now, angry that she had been intimidated, and at the same time beginning to feel the glow of victory.

She passed Grandfather's still form, pausing a moment to make certain that no wisp of dirty fog remained to hide there. She must not overlook that possibility. That was the hiding place from which it had leaped at White Fox. She lifted the torch and thrust it into the shallow recess, driving out the shadows.

Giving this opportunity, she expected an attack from the ledge, and was ready. There was a rush of the shapeless mass, and a terrifying hiss. It was like the hiss of the fat-bodied blunt-nosed snake, who is harmless but threatens mightily. She smiled to herself as she swung the firebrand back, to thrust at the dark fog. *I know you now,* she thought. *You are all wind, and threatening, like the blow-snake, but no danger to us. We know you now.*

The Thing recoiled, and seemed to draw in upon itself, then began again to slither backward, up and toward the cave. South Wind pursued it relentlessly, thrusting at it with her torch, moving faster now. She could hear the reassuring beat of the drum from below, and the now hoarse voice of White Fox, as he attempted to maintain the song. A little longer, Fox, she thought, just a little more.

Into the cave crept the dirty brown of the Thing, and she thought it seemed smaller already.

"Back," she demanded aloud, pointing to the crevice.

There was one more perfunctory rush, another threatening hiss, but she parried the thrust with the firebrand. The dark fog began to disappear into the crevice, like water flowing down a hole in the ground. There was one last feeble hiss and it was gone.

South Wind looked around the chamber that had been her lodge for as long as she could remember. It was in disarray, the willow racks toppled and crushed, small possessions broken or scattered. It could be restored to livable condition, but . . . she nudged a broken willow stick with her toe. The racks, the backrests, all would have to be rebuilt. First, this must be finished.

She stooped and began to pick up the broken willow sticks, now dry and brittle. Still carrying the cedar torch in her right hand, she began to thrust the dry sticks into the crevice. With increasing emotion, almost a burning anger, she continued, cramming the dark hole with the remnants of her past.

With the broken fragments now packed in and over the crevice, like the disorderly lodge of a pack rat, she took a step back and surveyed her work by the light of her dying torch. Then she thrust the cedar knot into the center of the pile.

*Die, Evil One,* she thought.

Little tongues of flame began to lick at the tinder-dry willow sticks. Dense white smoke wandered for a moment in the uncertain air, and then began to find its way upward, to disappear into the smoke-hole above. The heat began to fill the cave, and South Wind retreated to the cool outside air of the ledge.

She took a deep breath, and looked for a moment upriver. Sun Boy had painted the sky in honor of his leaving, and dusk had not quite settled over the Rock. Below, the rhythm of the drum still sounded.

"White Fox," she shouted. "It is over. It is dead."

There was a pause.

"Are you sure?" he called hoarsely.

"Yes, yes!"

Tears were streaming down her face, feeling hot at first, but quickly fanned to coolness by the night breeze. Downriver, the arc of the full moon was just peering over Earth's rim. It was a night of victory, of great and powerful medicine. She must hurry down, to share it with White Fox.

"I am coming down," she called.

Behind her, the fire in the cave was roaring now, crackling as it purified. The cave would be clean again, free of the tainted odor of decay and stagnation, ready to start a new life. As soon as White Fox's leg was healed, they would come back up to live.

She paused and knelt to make hand-signs to Grandfather.

"We have killed the Evil One, Grandfather. It is gone!"

She jumped to her feet and hurried on down the path, across the sand of the beach, and through the riffle.

"Fox!" she exclaimed. "We did it! It is dead!"

She knelt to give him a quick hug, careful not to bump the injured leg, and then moved to build up the fire.

"Are you sure?" he asked insistently. "Tell me . . . what happened?"

His voice was so hoarse that he could hardly talk, from the long evening in which he had held the Thing at bay with the drum and the chant. South Wind hurried back and dropped beside him, like a delighted child.

"It is good!" she exclaimed, laughing, the beautiful liquid sound that he had not heard for many days.

In signs and words, she related her story.

"You saw most of it. I drove it up the path with the torch, into the cave and down the hole, then made a big fire in the cave, in the hole."

"Are you sure?" he croaked again. "There are no scraps along the cliff?"

"No, no," she assured him. "But it does not matter. It cannot live now. We *know* about it. We have killed it, Fox!"

She gave him another quick hug.

"Now we can begin to plan," she told him. "The cave will be cool in a day or two. I will clean it out, sweep the ashes, and we will rebuild the racks. How long until I can help you back up there?"

White Fox hesitated a moment, then started to speak, but abandoned it in favor of sign talk.

"Wind, we must think of many things. It will be many sleeps before I could go up there. We must have shelter. It may rain. There were many colors tonight." He pointed to the glow that still hung in the west. "The birds flew low today. There could be rain soon."

"Then we must move," she told him. "In the morning. The river rises quickly."

"I cannot go up the cliff."

"Then we will go somewhere else," she told him. "We can do *anything* now, Fox. We have won!"

# 32

>> >> >>

"**W**ell, you did it. You finally thought it out. But the girl saved you."

The voice of the little gnome-like man came from somewhere above him. White Fox raised his head to look, but saw nothing.

"Where are you?" he asked. "Show yourself. It is hard to talk to someone I cannot see."

There was a mocking laugh from above.

"You still do not believe, even now? Ah, well . . ."

There he sat, on a large horizontal limb of the sycamore, head cocked to the side in the familiar way. He was swinging his feet, and White Fox could even see the decorative thongs on the heels of the little moccasins as they fluttered back and forth. Fox was certain that there had been nothing on the limb a moment ago.

South Wind had gone to select a place for them on the hillside, above the level of a possible flash flood on the river. They had spent another sleepless night, this time not from fear but from the excitement of victory. Again and again, they recounted for each other the little details of the experience from each point of view. South Wind related how the fog had crept down the crevice, and how she had pursued it with the fire and destroyed it.

He, in turn, told of his fears when the brown mist seemed to break in pieces and began to crawl over the ledge. Then they would laugh and hug each other again for joy.

"We fought the Thing and killed it, Fox!" she said over and over.

"Do you want to make a song about it?" he asked. "That is our way, to tell it to others in a song."

She shook her head, embarrassed.

"I could not sing to others. Only to you."

"It is not hard," he urged. "You will learn."

She shot a quick glance at him, but said nothing. He did not pursue it further, for the moment. He noticed with pleasure, though, that she did not entirely deny the possibility of contact with other people. They would talk, later.

So far, they had spoken of no plans beyond that of moving to higher ground. That, for the moment, seemed a major task. He was sure that he could be of little or no help. He could crawl only a short distance, and she could not carry him. She had dragged him up the ledge, when she first captured him, but he had been unconscious at the time, and he now had an injured leg which would complicate matters. Maybe he could crawl a little way, then rest, and crawl again.

First, of course, they must choose a place to go. With that in mind, South Wind had gone to look, leaving him at the fire.

It was then that the little man who called himself Small Fox had returned. White Fox was grateful that he seldom appeared while the girl was present. That had been a tense moment.

"Small Fox, we are thankful for your help."

" 'We'? You have told the girl? *Aiee*, does she think you crazy?"

He knew that the little man was mocking him. It was probable that Small Fox knew every word, maybe every thought that had passed between them.

"No, but you know what I mean."

"Do I? Do you really believe, now?" the little man teased.

"Of course. But tell me more. Do you have a wife?"

There was a startled look on the small face, and he began to laugh so hard that White Fox thought again he would fall.

"Not yet," the little man said finally. "But soon, maybe."

"Will I see her?"

"Maybe. Maybe you will not even see me!"

"But I do not understand. You came to help me."

"Did I?"

"Of course!"

The gnome-like figure vanished, and only the voice was apparent.

"Did I help you? Or did you only help yourself?" The voice was mocking again. *"Aiee*, Fox, maybe you are stupid after all."

"But you came and talked to me."

"Are you sure? What do you have to make you think so? Maybe I am *not* real, but only in your head."

"But I *saw* you!"

Small Fox was back again, standing on the limb and leaning against the trunk of the sycamore.

"The girl did not," he taunted. "Why? Am I only in *your* head, maybe?"

White Fox's head was spinning. Was he going crazy? First, the little man had insisted on his reality, and now seemed determined to deny it. Now he chuckled.

"You may be crazy," he said, in answer to the unasked question, "but that is another matter. Think, now, do you have anything to prove I am real? You have never touched me."

"I have never touched the wind," White Fox observed, "but it is real."

*"Ah*, you *do* begin to see. You do not have to *understand*, for it to be real."

"Are you in my mind, then?"

"Of course. You are talking to me."

"No, I mean, are you *only* in my mind?"

"What would be the purpose in knowing that? Does it matter?"

"I . . . I guess not. What about the Thing, in the Rock? Is it dead?"

The little man laughed.

"Was it ever alive?"

"But we *both* saw it, South Wind and I."

"Yes. It was in both minds."

"But nowhere else?"

"*Aiee*, Fox, why must you . . . look, is the wind real?"

"Of course."

"Do you understand it?"

"No."

There were many things he did not understand, he realized. Many that he was unlikely to. Understanding had little to do with reality. He would talk to Looks Far, who understood more of such things. Maybe, even, it was a matter of understanding that one need not understand.

He regretted that he had not had opportunity to use more of the teachings of Looks Far. An idea began to grow. He *could* apprentice himself to the medicine man. He had a successful vision-quest, a powerful spirit-guide. It seemed that there was every reason to think that the medicine man would help him.

The little man on the limb was smiling.

"That is a good thought!" he remarked.

"Will you help . . ."

"*Aiee*, there you go, again! You ask my help, yet are not sure whether I am only in your mind."

He began to fade. White Fox smiled. It was an amusing game, one which might never be finished, or might already be over. But, he now realized, it need not worry him. He would not, he decided, tell anyone about the little man. Well, possibly Looks Far, who would certainly understand. The outlines of the figure on the limb were gone now, but a mocking little voice sounded from the leafy canopy.

"Ask yourself," it taunted, "why we have the same name!"

White Fox laughed aloud.

"What did you say?" asked South Wind.

She had a pair of young rabbits slung over her shoulder, and was smiling.

"What? Oh, nothing," he said. "I was talking to myself."

"Oh. I found a place for us to stay," she said, dropping the rabbits and her bow. "Shall we eat first?"

"It does not matter," he said. "I will help you clean the rabbits, while you tell me about it."

# 33

**》》》**

"**W**hile the meat cooks," she signed, "I will go back to the cave. There may be something there that we can use."

She used hand-signs, because it was easier for her than word-talk, and this was a difficult morning. She was curious about the cave.

"You are not afraid?" White Fox asked.

"No. It is over, Fox, but I want to see the cave again."

This was a big day in her life, and she was filled with uncertainty. Nothing would ever be the same again. She realized now that her thoughts of living in the cave with White Fox were childish daydreams. That could not happen. But she was uncertain what could. She wished with all her heart to live with this young man who had returned to help her. At great risk to himself, she knew now. She thought that he felt the same, but they had never talked about it.

They had been so happy in the long sunny afternoons, swimming in the river, drying in the sun on the white sandy shore, and laughing together. She had known, in her heart, that they could not simply do this always, could not live forever this way. But she had no experience to tell her what else the world offered. Her world had been the Rock, with all its rugged beauty, with its closeness to things of the spirit, the cave's warm protection in the Moon of Snows. She was afraid, at the thought of living elsewhere. It would help, of course, to be with White Fox, and she thought he wanted that, too. Soon she must ask him about it.

First, she wanted to see the cave once more. It was the only home she had ever known. She did not think she could ever *live* there again, but she felt a need, somehow, to take a last look, to say good-bye.

She must also say good-bye to Grandfather. They were not leaving immediately, only moving to a cleft in the rocky shelf across the river. But, it called her attention to the fact that sometime, they would leave. This left her with an unanswered question. What would become of Grandfather? He had instructed her carefully in the immediate care of the dead, but what then? She knew, from experience, that dead things decay. She had seen the body of a deer that she had found dead in the woods. Over a period of time, its flesh returned to the earth, and the bones whitened, and were scattered. Grandfather had explained that this was the way of all things. The grass grows, to nourish the rabbit, deer and buffalo, which in turn feed the fox, the hawk, the wolf, and man. They, in their time, return to the earth, and the circle starts again.

She did not understand, however, exactly how the bones of man return to earth. He had not gone that far in his explanation. An idea occurred to her now, as she started up to the cave, and she turned back. Fox would know.

"Fox," she asked in signs, "what happens to your dead?"

He looked up, puzzled.

"What? They are wrapped, like your grandfather. Usually in a tree or on a scaffold."

"Yes, Grandfather told me. But after that. They do not stay there forever."

"Oh. Sometimes, the next season, maybe, we would carry the bones, still wrapped, or gathered together, to bury them."

"In the ground?"

"Yes. Or cover them with stones. The spirit has crossed over already, and the flesh returns . . ."

"Yes, I know," she interrupted, as she turned away.

She felt better, now. She knew what she would do. There would be some time, while Fox's leg healed, when she could come up the path, and work a little at a time.

She picked up a rock from beside the path and carried it with her. It was heavy, and several times she stopped to set it down and rest. When she came to the still form on the ledge, she placed it carefully, and rose to sign her greeting. Then she turned to the boulder where she had sat so many times. She managed to push it over, and rolled it once again, into position.

South Wind studied what she had accomplished, picked up a smaller boulder and added it to the wall she was beginning. She nodded and smiled. Yes, it would not take long. Each time she came up, she would place a few stones, and soon Grandfather would be protected from further exposure to the elements.

The girl walked on up to the cave, confident now. The roof was blackened inside, and tiny wisps of white smoke still rose from the heap of white ash in the back of the cave. It was clean, burned clean and purified by the fire of last night. It was good.

She looked around the little cave. It looked smaller, somehow, than it once had. It held many memories of times good and bad, but would never hold the fear again that had nearly overwhelmed her in the past few moons. She turned away, a little sadly.

South Wind made her way back down the ledge, pausing to lift a pumpkin-sized rock to add to Grandfather's cairn. Then, on down to cross the river. Sometime, she would tell White Fox what she had contrived for the remains of Grandfather, but not now.

"The meat is ready," he called as she approached. "Is the cave safe?"

"Yes, it is good. There is nothing there, but it is clean."

She used signs, and wondered a little at her choice of the sign for "clean." But no, it *was* clean, burned and purified, all trace of the dirty brown fog destroyed. She shuddered a little, but felt confident and happy now.

Sitting beside him, she told him of their temporary lodge while they ate.

"It is about a bow shot away, there in the rocks. We can stretch a robe over the top, across the cleft. It faces north, but we will be out by winter."

She paused and looked at him.

"Where will we be?"

"Where do you want to be?" he asked.

"With you . . . I . . ."

She stopped, a feeling of panic rushing over her. She realized that she had just suggested, by implication, that they rejoin his people. She was not certain she was ready for that.

"With my people?" he asked cautiously.

South Wind's heart was racing. She was afraid. All her life, she had feared people. She was not sure that she could tolerate the presence of many others in close proximity.

"I do not know, Fox," she said. "Tell me again of your father and mother."

He began to tell her stories of his childhood, of his mother's comforting touch and his father's instruction. Of the instruction he had received in the Rabbit Society, where each member of the tribe instructed the children in that which he knew best.

"It seems like having many grandfathers," she said in wonder.

"Yes!" he agreed. "It is like that. Like many people to help and teach and comfort when you are hurt or sad."

Maybe, she thought, maybe she could learn.

"Are there no evil people? Grandfather said . . ."

"Yes, sometimes. But there are more who will help, so you do not have to run and hide."

"You would be with me?"

"Of course."

She was facing him, and as he spoke, she saw a motion beyond him, just over the rim of the nearby hill.

"Fox!" she gasped. "People! They are coming!"

She jumped to her feet to run. White Fox turned quickly to look. A horseman now became visible, closely followed by others.

"*Aiee!*" White Fox shouted, laughing, "it is my Father . . . my Mother, too. Father! Over here!"

In a few moments the newcomers had rushed forward, and everyone was swinging down from the horses.

South Wind was frightened. She would have run to hide, but she stubbornly refused to leave White Fox. Instead, she took a stance directly behind him, suspiciously watching those who approached. Soon, everyone was laughing and talking all at once, and hugging each other. South Wind withdrew a step or two, and watched.

These people did not look dangerous. Fox trusted them. No one tried to threaten her, or even approach her. Their main attitude seemed to be one of friendly curiosity.

There were three men, one a bit older than the others. That one reminded her of her grandfather, as she remembered him when she was small, before his mind became confused. She guessed that he must be White Fox's father.

The woman must be the mother of White Fox. She hugged him with tears in her eyes. South Wind had never seen a woman before. At least, not up close like this. She had a warm, friendly smile, and her face, as she looked at South Wind, was gentle and understanding. It might be good to talk with her of woman-things.

The girl wondered if this person looked like the mother that she did not remember. She hoped so.

# 34

>> >> >>

**W**hen it was all over, very few among the People ever heard the story. Even among the Elk-dog band, only the part about the long-lost girl, located and brought home as a wife by one of their young men, was known to all.

The young warriors who had accompanied White Fox's parents on the search understood that there was some sort of vision involved. Looks Far had cast the bones and wished them well. The corpse on the ledge, cared for by the girl, and carefully covered before they left, was not especially unusual. They felt sympathy for her, left alone by her grandfather's death. Perhaps, as they cut poles for the travois to carry the injured White Fox home, their main thought was for his good fortune. His leg would heal, but *aiee*, how fortunate he was, to have found such a beauty.

South Wind was quite possibly the most beautiful woman either of them had ever seen. They could not avoid noticing the way she hovered over the injured Fox, or her adoring expression as she looked at him.

"Ah, how would you feel to have such a woman look at you like that?" one asked the other.

"It might be worth a broken leg!"

They both chuckled.

"Fox was always lucky."

Red Feather and Moonflower were completely charmed by the girl. Moonflower, especially, was touched by sympathy. She, herself, had been forced to adjust to a strange culture when she married Red Feather. She could understand some of the girl's problems, though not in any way the reclusive life with the grandfather, or the tragedy of his loss. Her heart went out to the girl.

Custom would have decreed that the newly married couple live in the home of the bride's mother until they completed their own lodge, but South Wind had no mother. Moonflower opened not only her heart but her lodge. There were even jokes that if the newcomer's husband did not treat her well, *his* mother would come to her defense.

Red Feather was proud, as proud as any father whose son has married well. He was pleased that the girl seemed to accept him as the father she had never had. He was also pleased and proud when White Fox announced that he would become the apprentice of Looks Far. *Aiee,* Fox could become one of the greatest medicine men in the history of the tribe. It was good.

The one who perhaps came closer to understanding the whole story than anyone was, of course, Looks Far. He watched the little procession as they came home, the injured White Fox riding on the pole-drag. He could not have been more pleased at Fox's inquiry about a career in his own footsteps.

The young people were married, and the entire band rejoiced with them in their happiness. They seemed perfectly matched to each other, and continued so.

In time, both found that their occasional night-dreams ceased to bother them. They shared a part of their experiences with Looks Far, but some they never told to anyone. The unpleasant memories quickly faded, and by the time their first child was born, sometimes it seemed that the events at the Rock had never happened at all.

Years later, White Fox tried to tell his wife about the strange little gnome-like man, but she only laughed, and accused him of teasing her.

# GENEALOGY

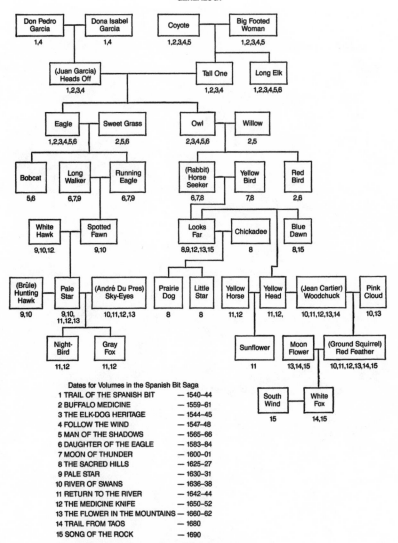

Dates for Volumes in the Spanish Bit Saga

1 TRAIL OF THE SPANISH BIT — 1540–44
2 BUFFALO MEDICINE — 1559–61
3 THE ELK-DOG HERITAGE — 1544–45
4 FOLLOW THE WIND — 1547–48
5 MAN OF THE SHADOWS — 1565–66
6 DAUGHTER OF THE EAGLE — 1583–84
7 MOON OF THUNDER — 1600–01
8 THE SACRED HILLS — 1625–27
9 PALE STAR — 1630–31
10 RIVER OF SWANS — 1636–38
11 RETURN TO THE RIVER — 1642–44
12 THE MEDICINE KNIFE — 1650–52
13 THE FLOWER IN THE MOUNTAINS — 1660–62
14 TRAIL FROM TAOS — 1680
15 SONG OF THE ROCK — 1690

Dates are only approximate, since the People have no written calendar.
Characters in the Genealogy appear in the volumes indicated.

DON COLDSMITH, a former president of the Western Writers of America, writes a syndicated column on horses, and is a breeder of Appaloosas. Other novels in his Spanish Bit Saga include *Pale Star, The Sacred Hills, Moon of Thunder,* and *Return to the River.* Mr. Coldsmith lives near Emporia, Kansas.